Eternal Peace

Copyright © Stephanie Owens, 2011. All rights reserved. No part of this book may be reproduced or transmitted in any form or by any means, electronic or mechanical, including photocopying, recording, or by any information storage and retrieval system, without permission in writing from the publisher.

Bedside Books
An imprint of American Book Publishing
5442 So. 900 East, #146
Salt Lake City, UT 84117-7204
www.american-book.com
Printed in the United States of America on acid-free paper.

Eternal Peace

Designed by Jana Rade, design@american-book.com

Publisher's Note: This is a work of fiction. Names, characters, places, and incidents either are the product of the author's imagination, or are used fictitiously, and any resemblance to actual persons, living or dead, events, or locales is entirely coincidental.

ISBN-13: 978-1-58982-798-1
ISBN-10: 1-58982-798-8

Owens, Stephanie, Eternal Peace

Special Sales

These books are available at special discounts for bulk purchases. Special editions, including personalized covers, excerpts of existing books, and corporate imprints, can be created in large quantities for special needs. For more information e-mail info@american-book.com.

Eternal Peace

Stephanie Owens

Dedication

In loving memory of Grandma Faye Eversole.
(April 8, 1928 – October 26, 2009)

Who always listened to my stories no matter how ridiculous they were.
Love you always.

Prologue
Present Day

Devon Baxter looked back upon a past filled with regret. Standing beside his mother's grave Devon wished he had Roxie to share his grief with, she would understand the turmoil inside him. Roxie Lancaster could always lift his spirits in the darkest of times. His regret was not holding on to her when he'd had the chance, of not telling her that he loved her. He had always held back: for one fact, because they had been best friends for as long as he could remember. Devon had been afraid that the friendship they had shared would end, evolving into something different something that he hadn't been prepared for. Geez, he'd been young, they both had been.

He wished she were here today to help him make it through burying his mother. Devon was sure that Roxie would also be able to help him hold his father up against the grief that was already consuming him. Devon was completely alone and didn't know how to cope with these new changes except for what he always did, and that was to keep all of the pain inside. He mentally shook himself out of his reverie and realized that the funeral ceremony was almost over. His beautiful, laughing mother would no longer be coming home to him and his father. Three days ago Lilly was killed when a truck crossed into her lane on her way to the grocery store; it totaled both vehicles, destroying a family in the process.

After the final prayer was said, Devon helped his father to his feet and escorted him back to the waiting limousine that would take them home. Although both men looked similar with dark hair and penetrating, if unusual, green eyes, they were always at odds thanks to their same, strong personality. It was Lilly who held them together; she always found a kind word for anybody. Devon and his father rode home in silence. Their ranch, Bar B Ranch, was located in Peace, Oklahoma and was several thousand acres large, making it easy for the two to avoid each other for days on end. When they arrived at the ranch, Devon's father left the car almost before it had stopped and went straight to his room without a word to his son. Devon was in no hurry to get home. He knew that his memories would assail him as soon as he stepped over the threshold of the big two-story ranch house.

He went straight to his office. Located at the back of the house, Devon's office was a large room with a fireplace and a mini library of beloved assorted books; it also contained the one thing he needed more than anything else, a liquor cabinet and shot glasses. Devon picked up a whiskey bottle and glass and settled into the large chair that was situated in front of the roaring fireplace. Thankfully the housekeeper had kept the fire going; the weather was so cold outside. It would be a new year in a few days and he hoped the next one would be considerably better than the last one. Devon leaned back, letting the pain slide away and remembered a better time.

Chapter 1
Eleven Years Ago

The Lancaster ranch was set a few miles from the Bar B Ranch; although it was smaller it was still a prosperous cattle ranch. The Lancasters were like a second family to Devon. As far back as he could remember he had ridden over to the Lancaster's ranch on his horse. Roxie, the daughter of Lou and Milly Lancaster, would meet him in the barnyard. She would saddle her horse and they would ride out on the range to check the fences or the cattle. The two were always together.

They were both eighteen and had their whole lives ahead of them; Devon would be attending Oklahoma State University in the fall with a major in Agriculture Business and was having no luck convincing Roxie to join him in Stillwater. Roxie didn't want to go to college, but Devon just couldn't imagine being separated from his best friend, his soul mate, although he would never tell her that.

The sound of Roxie's voice brought Devon back to reality. Noticing that Devon hadn't been listening, Roxie looked at him strangely and asked again, "Are you staying for supper tonight?"

"Of course. Have I ever turned down one of your mama's meals?"

"No, but you seemed different this evening. I didn't know if you were feeling well and maybe wanted to go home," Roxie said not wanting to pry.

"Well I was thinking about college, you and the future. Have you thought anymore about coming with me?" Devon asked, hoping she had changed her mind.

Roxie gave a big sigh and looked from the back of her buckskin horse off toward the horizon. She didn't say anything for the longest time.

Finally Roxie turned to Devon and gave him a big smile that almost knocked him off his horse. He always loved to see her smile at him like that, except for the fact that she always followed it with some equally shocking statement; this time was no different. She said, "If you can give me one good reason to go with you then my answer is yes, but if you can't then I can't go with you."

Just like Devon thought, she wanted what he couldn't give… his love to her in words. He didn't respond except to give her a smile before turning away.

Four months later Devon was at college alone. Roxie went to visit her cousins in England. Devon never got the chance to give Roxie the reason to stay with him because she never came back, choosing to stay in England. Devon was later told that Roxie decided to travel the world making money doing odd jobs along the way.

Chapter 2
Present Day

Milly Lancaster missed her daughter so much that at times it felt like there was a hole in her heart. She knew why Roxie didn't come home and wished she could fix the problem. Roxie was, and would always be, in love with Devon Baxter. However, Roxie thought Devon didn't love her back. It had been eleven years since the Devon and Roxie had gone their separate ways. Sadly, it had also been eleven years since Milly and Lou had seen their daughter.

It was such a sad time. A week ago Roxie had refused to come home for Christmas for the millionth time, and then there was the death of Devon's sweet mama. Milly hadn't had the heart to call Roxie and tell her yet. If only she could think of a way to bring her daughter home. Even if it was only for a short visit, she knew she could get Devon and Roxie together. Then maybe Roxie would settle down and realize that Devon had always loved her, even if she didn't know it before she left.

Milly knew how much Roxie meant to Devon. It was obvious. Every weekend since Roxie had left, Devon had visited from school and inquired after her. He had tried to seem casual enough, but Milly knew better. He was hoping that Roxie would come home. They all were.

Eternal Peace

After four years of weekend visits, Devon finally accepted that Roxie wasn't coming back and that he would never get to see her again. It broke Milly's heart to remember that time when he had stood on their porch after coming from his college graduation. Roxie had sent her congratulations to Devon, but added not to expect her to come home. That was the first and only time Milly had seen Devon break down and cry in front of them; since that day it was as if Devon became a harder man that never let anyone know what he was thinking. He was never one to show emotions, but it became even worse after that day. Devon never even cried at his mama's funeral and, in Milly's opinion, all that pent up emotion was going to need a release someday and she was going to make sure she was the one that helped him finally do it. She was getting her daughter to come home so that Devon and Roxie could have it out once and for all.

She was still smiling over her plan when her husband came into the kitchen. Lou looked at his wife, saw the smile and knew something was up. He already didn't want to be involved. Anything that made Milly smile like that, especially when she had just come home from a friend's funeral, was not something he wanted to be a part of.

Feeling resigned, he knew he was going to ask anyway.

"So what's the smile for and what plan are cooking up in your head?" Lou asked.

Milly looked slyly at her husband and said, "I'm going to give our daughter a reason to come home."

Lou winced as he heard this statement; his daughter was a sore spot with him. He loved her so much and she still refused to come home even to see them.

"So how are you going to accomplish that? I mean short of telling her that something has happened to Devon…" As soon as Lou said it, he knew that was what his wife was about. "You can't call her and tell her something happened to Devon when it's not true."

"I'm not going to come out and say anything happened to Devon exactly... I'm just going to tell her that there was a car accident, that Devon's mama died, and that he is in critical condition and needs her."

Lou rolled his eyes. Critical condition indeed; the only critical part of it all was horrible grief the boy must be experiencing. This was just plain wrong, but he knew that once Milly had her mind made up there was no stopping her. "Fine, but when this all hits the fan, do not include me in this scheme." He turned and left the kitchen before she could tell him any more of her plan. He hoped his daughter would finally come home and stay once and for all, but he knew that would be too much to ask this late in the game.

Milly turned away from the stove where she was cooking dinner and reached for the phone. A moment later she was talking to Roxie.

"Hi mom, it's good to hear from you; it's been a whole week. Are you going to ask me to come home again because you know it won't do you any good," Roxie stated.

It was just like her daughter to cut to the point with hardly a proper hello. Milly knew she was going to have to stay balanced and levelheaded to keep the pretense going.

"No dear, I'm wouldn't dream of asking you to come home again, but I am calling to impart some sad news; then you can go back to whatever dead-end job you are it this time." Just like she hoped, there was a pause and then a reserved reply.

"Go on. I'm listening, mom."

"There was a car accident a few days ago and a good friend and neighbor died; it was Lilly Baxter. We attended her funeral today."

The silence on the other end of the line was deafening and then sobs could be heard as grief overtook her daughter. For a second Milly almost backed out of her original plan to deceive her, but decided she wanted to see her daughter more and this seemed to be the only way to accomplish that...as well as see Roxie and Devon finally together. Finally after a few minutes of tears and then hiccups being heard on the other line, Milly heard the question that would change everything.

"How's Devon doing with all this?"

"Well Honey, that's why this call is so hard to make; he's in critical condition and it's going to take something great to bring him out of it." Milly had to bite her tongue on the lie. She was nervous and silently promised herself that she would say extra prayers of forgiveness for telling her daughter this obvious stretch of the truth.

"NO NOT DEVON! Are you telling me he was in the accident, mom? Why didn't you call me sooner?" Roxie asked frantically.

"Well Honey, I didn't think it would make any difference to you. You've told us numerous times you weren't coming home," Milly stated matter-of-factly.

"Yes mom, but you knew the reason why I didn't come home. I can't believe Devon's been hurt and his mom is gone now. What about John? Was he also in the accident?" Roxie asked.

"No, he was out on the ranch working when he got the news about the accident. Well, I just wanted you to know since you were close to their family at one time," Milly said, trying to sound distant. More silence greeted her, but she wasn't giving up yet.

"Mom, I need some time to think. If you don't mind, I'll talk to you some other time, bye." Before Milly could say anything else her daughter had already hung up the phone.

New York City

Sitting on her couch in the apartment that she was so proud of, Roxie saw nothing; she just felt numb after the shock that her mom had just delivered. She had planned on never going back to Peace, Oklahoma and her parent's ranch that she loved so much. She had planned on never going back because of Devon Baxter. Knowing that she would always love him and that he would never return the feelings broke her heart. She had given him a chance eleven years ago on that long ago summer day and, even then, he couldn't tell her how he felt about her. She knew he cared about her. They had been best friends for so long that it was impossible for him not to have some feelings for her. That didn't make it any easier. She had always hoped that he would come after her... that he would show her how much he had always loved her, but he obviously just didn't care enough.

It had been an exceptionally hard day today at work and then, to top everything off, the call from her mother had come. Roxie was completely exhausted. She fell asleep the moment her head touched her pillow.

The next morning Roxie gradually opened her eyes to discover that she had slept late because she hadn't fallen asleep until well after midnight. She felt like she had sandpaper for eyelids. Laying on her back in her massive king size bed, she came up with the decision that would take her back to her past and maybe a new future. After her morning routine she opened her laptop and proceeded to make plane reservations that would leave in a few hours for Oklahoma.

A last minute plane ticket would have cost her a fortune had she actually lived the life that she had convinced everyone she was living. In actuality, Roxie had made a small fortune as an investment banker. She didn't really understand why she kept this from her parents, just that she thought if she distanced herself from anything back home it would be easier somehow.

So when her parents, or anyone else for that matter, asked how she was doing out on her own, she made up a story about how she was traveling and working odd jobs. The truth was that Roxie had become a millionaire doing what she had always done best, being spontaneous. So with that in mind, she had to rethink her plan and arrive as the poor relation that she was instead of arriving in her little black sports car that she loved. She almost hated to leave the car in storage, but she was truly concerned about Devon's condition and wanted to get there as quickly as possible. She knew

Eternal Peace

that she could only do that by flying, not driving. With everything planned and her bags packed she had too much time to reflect, so instead she called her office and made plans to take an extended vacation. She'd let them know that she could be reached by phone and e-mail on any important decisions that needed to be made.

Three hours later Roxie was on the plane and trying to steady her nerves. It wasn't helping anything that the man sitting next to her in the first class section kept trying to hit on her. She knew that she wasn't bad to look at, but sheesh what was the deal? She had natural Honey-blond hair and whiskey colored eyes, that even she had to admit were unusual, but she considered those her only saving grace. Blissfully, sleep claimed her thirty minutes later taking her away from her worrisome thoughts of Devon and the annoying man beside her.

Landing in Oklahoma City, Roxie hurried through the airport to find her luggage and make it to her bus on time. The bus would drop her through Peace where she could call her parents to pick her up. Hopefully they would come and get her; after all the times she had turned them down to come home, she wasn't so sure they wouldn't just leave her at the bus stop. Oh well, this was the only solution she had. It was an hour bus ride to the quiet town of Peace, so that put her arriving about one o'clock in the afternoon. That would give her time to check on Devon at the hospital before calling her parents, grabbing a shower, and then returning to the hospital to stay with Devon until he made a recovery good enough that she felt it safe enough to leave him.

Settling in her seat on the bus, Roxie blocked out everything and only thought about what she would say to Devon when she saw him again. She only hoped his being in critical condition wouldn't last much longer; it would be hard enough seeing him in pain, but not knowing if he would make it would kill something inside of her that she knew she would never recover from.

Roxie had been through her fair share of bad situations. After all, traveling the world often meant getting into some sort of trouble.

However, in the weeks to come, her strength and faith would be tested beyond her wildest imagination; it wouldn't be only from seeing Devon again, but from things far out of her control.

Chapter 3

A few hours later Roxie stepped out from the bus and looked around her old hometown. The nostalgia was overwhelming. She didn't think she would have missed seeing everything so much and maybe it wouldn't have been so bad, but nothing had changed in Peace in the eleven years she had been absent.

Turning to her right, after gathering her luggage, she pulled her cell phone from her back pocket to call her parents to see if they would come and pick her up. She was just starting to dial the number when she heard a diesel engine shut off. Glancing up Roxie spotted a bright red Ford pickup and stepping from the truck was the most gorgeous man she had ever laid eyes on. He was easily six foot three and was wearing the garb of a ranch Cowboy, with dark shades over his eyes.

Roxie couldn't believe it. He looked just like Devon! She could feel chills skittering down her spine. Then, as if the suspense was killing her, he removed the shades and glanced her way. They both froze for what seemed an eternity.

At first Devon thought he was hallucinating. It couldn't possibly be Roxie. She had told her parents that she was never coming home.

The woman started running towards him, yelling his name over and over. Devon was still wondering what the hell was going on, when the next thing he knew she had jumped into his arms, wrapped her legs around his waist and gave him the kiss of his life. Then it registered that it truly was Roxie and, for whatever reason she had, Roxie had come home. He started kissing her in earnest. The only thought floating through his mind was: "damn, this woman can kiss."

When both of them came up for air it was to the realization that everybody around them on the sidewalk was staring at them. While both Roxie and Devon tried to catch their breath, they both started talking at once.

"Mom said…"

"Your Mom said…"

"You go..."

"No, you go..."

They both stopped again and just started laughing. It was then that they both realized that Roxie's legs were still wrapped around Devon's waist. As the laughter died, Roxie slowly let go and slid down the length of Devon's body, but he refused to let her go completely.

"I can't believe you're out of the hospital so soon," Roxie said. She couldn't believe that Devon was standing in front of her.

Devon looked at her like she was crazy.

"What are you talking about?" Not bothering for an answer he said, "Forget it. Let's get in my truck and go somewhere and talk before we cause even more of a scene."

Without waiting for an answer, Devon took Roxie's luggage and threw it into the back of the truck, lifted her into the cab as if she couldn't do it herself, then rounded the truck, got in himself and took off out of town without saying another word to her.

She couldn't take her eyes off of Devon. Captured in the moment, she was about to ask him the first of hundreds of questions when she realized then that either her mom had lied to her to get her to come home or Devon had made the fastest recovery from a car accident than was humanly possible. She couldn't believe her mother had called her with the express purpose of lying to her about Devon just to get her to come home. Surely her mom wouldn't lie and tell her that Devon's mom had died in the accident. Devon looked liked he had been dragged to hell and back, so at least that much of the story was sadly true. When Devon took his sunglasses off she could see the grief in his eyes. He had lost the boyish innocence that he had once carried, leaving behind an older man with secrets of his own. She knew that she would need to be extremely sharp with this older version of the Devon that she knew and loved.

Devon shifted in his seat and tried to slow his racing thoughts. Darn it, what the hell was she doing back? She looked so good and kissed even better and he should be madder than hell that she had just come home where she truly belonged. What the hell had she meant about the hospital? Could she have heard about the accident and assumed that he had been involved? That didn't make any sense. The only people that could have told her would have been her parents and surely they would have told her the whole story. Unless she truly cared about him and hadn't listened to the whole story... maybe she had jumped on the first bus to get here just because she thought he was hurt and in the hospital. *Whoa boy, you're getting way ahead of yourself. You haven't seen Roxie in eleven years; she could just have come to see her parents.* Yeah, right. Roxie had a reason for being here; he only hoped it involved him somehow.

After twenty minutes of driving and no talking, but lots of glances at each other, the truck finally turned into a beautiful gate flanked by giant oak trees. It was another half a mile to the main ranch house, but Roxie remembered the place so well from her past and nothing had really changed.

When the truck finally came to a stop neither one of them bothered to get out. They just sat there and stared at each other for what seemed a lifetime. Finally, when the tension couldn't last any longer, Devon took a huge breath and asked, "What are you doing back and why did it take you so long to come home?"

It took several breaths for Roxie to find her voice, but she finally managed to answer Devon's question.

"I was told about the horrible car accident and about your mother and about you. I'm so sorry about your mother, Devon. I loved her like she was my own."

The mention of his mother brought on a new wave of grief and Devon dropped his forehead to the steering wheel to regain his composure before asking his next question.

"What about me? What was the remark at the bus stop about the hospital?"

"Mom called and told me about the accident, that your mom had been killed and that you were in critical condition and that it would take something extraordinary to get you to make a recovery," Roxie answered.

"So why didn't you come sooner for Mom's funeral and to see me if you thought I was in the hospital?"

"Mom called me less than ten hours ago with the news. I would have been here sooner had I known, and for the record why aren't you in the hospital? The injuries must have been extensive if the car accident was fatal for your mother."

Devon took a breath and realized that whatever reason Milly Lancaster had for lying to her daughter about the accident, he would also ask the Lord above to bless the woman for having the foresight to bring her daughter home to them and him.

"I wasn't in the accident, Roxie," Devon finally said after a moment.

"What do you mean? Mom said you were in critical condition." It couldn't be; her mom wouldn't lie to her about something like this, but as Roxie sat there and stared at Devon that was the only plausible explanation there was.

"Milly lied, Roxie. I can only assume that she had her reasons. Frankly, I'm flattered that my being injured would bring you home so quick when nothing else would," Devon said. He could feel his spirits lift at the thought that she'd come home because of him.

"Well don't be. I really came to see my parents not because I thought you were hurt," Roxie stated huffily.

Devon snorted. "Yeah, right. If that were the case you would have come home sooner. No, Roxie. Whatever reason you had for staying away, I know now that it involved me. Before you think of a way to leave and go traveling again, I will find a way to keep you here for good this time," Devon finished sounding determined.

Roxie paled, but lifted her chin defiantly and stared back at him.

"What I told you eleven years ago still stands. That is the only thing you can tell me to make me stay and I don't think you will ever let me get that close to you... or anyone for that matter, so it's water under the bridge at this point," she stated firmly. *There*, she thought. *I told him.*

"Yes, I remember and I might just surprise you, Roxie."

"That's doubtful. Let's drop this subject and start one that has meaning. Since I'm here for a few days why not help me to get back at my parents for the trick they played on us?"

"What do you have in mind exactly?" Devon asked warily. He knew that smirk all too well. He also knew that the next few days wouldn't be boring if Roxie stayed anywhere in the vicinity.

Chapter 4

"Well how about me moving in with you for the next few days?" Roxie stated, trying to bite back a smile as Devon's mouth dropped open.

"Excuse me, I don't think I heard you right."

"Yes, you did. Mom and Dad don't realize that I'm home so let me move in. Then you can casually mention to my parents sometime when you see them in the next day or so that you have met an old friend from college and asked her to move in with you."

"What makes you think I will just run into your parents in the next day or so?"

"Please, if I know you and my mother you go there for dinner whenever you can."

Damn, she did know both of them well and she wasn't stupid. Devon looked out the windshield and thought of some way out of this; he didn't relish playing any kind of tricks on Milly and Lou Lancaster, but he would also do anything to keep Roxie as close to him for as long as possible.

Roxie knew she had him. They'd been friends for too many years for her not to know when Devon was sunk, but like any true man he kept trying to argue.

"Well okay, but what about today? Everybody in town saw you, especially kissing me the way you were; someone was bound to recognize you."

"It's been eleven years, Devon. When the story is told they won't remember details and you never said my name in front of anybody, so if it comes up you can wing it and act like she's the one moving in with you, which is technically the truth."

"I don't know Roxie."

Roxie just rolled her eyes and smiled.

Man, the woman had a smile. "Okay deal, but you have to stay at least a month before you think about leaving again." *The man knew how to make her squirm.* Roxie sighed.

"Can't we work something else out? Maybe two weeks?"

"No deal; a month or nothing."

She tried to wait him out. Maybe he would change his mind. What possible reason would he want her to stay here a month? After several minutes Devon finally broke the silence.

"That's the deal Roxie, take it or leave it."

"Fine, darn it, but I don't have to like it." With that she opened the truck door and stepped out onto the walkway that led up to the ranch house. Devon just smiled and took his time getting out of the truck. He walked around the bed of the truck and started unloading Roxie's luggage. It didn't seem like she had a whole lot to her name. He felt sad that after eleven years all she had was a couple of old duffel bags, and judging by the clothes she was wearing they seemed to be of Goodwill quality. He might just need to discreetly find a way to buy her some good clothes while she was staying with him.

As he entered the house, he waited for the normal grief to hit him about his mom, but although it was there it was somehow lessened with Roxie in the house. Devon had a renewed purpose in life and it was to keep her home this time, even if he only had a month to accomplish it.

As he carried the luggage up the stairs he could hear Roxie running to meet him. Breathless, she called out, "I just remembered... where's your dad at?"

"Dad left shortly after the funeral." From the set of Devon's jaw and the anger that suddenly came to his eyes, she knew she wouldn't get any other answer than that. On the up side, it would be one less person to know of the charade for a while, but the down side was that they would have the entire house to their selves, which could turn out to be potentially dangerous to her sanity because she didn't know if she would be able to keep her hands off Devon. Well she wouldn't let this get in the way of anything. She could play it cool and let him know this wouldn't affect her in any way.

"You could have at least told me that your father wouldn't be in the house before making the deal with me. I would have renegotiated the terms of the deal."

Devon wasn't fooled. He just smiled up at Roxie at the top of the stairs and drawled, "But it was so much funnier this way." With that he pushed past her and went to put her things in an extra guestroom, one that would be directly across from his master suite. Yes, if he had his way she would be sharing his room before long.

Roxie hadn't moved from the top of the stairs when Devon came back from the bedroom, walked past her again and proceeded to go about his business. Then he turned and looked at her and smirked. "Well let's go talk about this plan of yours against your parents, that is if you aren't too chicken to go along with it now, knowing the situation is different now."

Roxie just snorted and proceeded to walk down the stairs and right up to Devon. She stood so close that his breathing hitched a little from the proximity. Lord, she smelled just like wildflowers, just like he remembered. Then he caught the twinkle in her eye and, smiling, she said, "Bring it on, big boy. I can handle anything you throw at me."

He just bet she could too.

Eternal Peace

Roxie turned and left him standing there. *Let him recover from that,* she thought.

It definitely didn't take Roxie long to make herself at home. As Devon walked into the kitchen, he found her rummaging through his fridge. She turned to find him staring at her.

"Well if we are going to hatch a plan then we need food," she said. "I'm starved."

They carried the assortment of foods from the fridge and pantry to the living room area and spread it all out on the coffee table. They each took a comfortable chair across from each other.

"So what's the plan, Rox? How do you expect me to keep your parents in the dark about you being back?" Devon asked, not really knowing how he was going to keep her presence on the ranch a secret.

"Just like I said earlier. I'll just stay out of town and let your ranch hands catch glimpses of me so that there will be a story of a woman staying at the great Bar B Ranch House. It will especially draw attention with no one else being in residence at the moment with your father gone on a trip and all. Basically when you see my parents just play it by ear," Roxie responded, acting as if this situation was completely normal.

"Well shoot Rox, I didn't realize it would be so easy. You've been gone for years, show up because your mom lied to you and now want me to follow right along with whatever plan you hatched up." Devon's voice rose till he was nearly shouting, but he didn't care anymore. He had eleven years of pent up frustration left in him to deal with. He just now was realizing how truly angry he was at her. "Darn it, Roxie. What about my mother? Who cares if your mom lied to you? She did it to get you to come home to her and your father. My mother will never walk through the front door again and tell me year after year that you will come home to all of us. That's what she did, by the way. She was always there for me, which is more than I can say for you. You chose to stay away all this time. Do you think you are the only one with any feelings? Hell no! You're selfish, Roxie!"

During his tirade Devon got up and had started pacing. He ended up with his back to Roxie; he was looking out the bay windows, his shoulders slumped.

He heard sobs coming from behind him and reflected on what he had just said. He could have cursed. Roxie had just come back and he had probably made her want to be anywhere else but in his living room at that moment. He turned to apologize and was struck by a body slamming into him and hugging his waist, sobs soaking his shirt.

"I'm so sorry Devon. You're right, I have been a selfish brat and I have no right to want to get back at my mom for lying to me. She and dad just wanted me to come home, but there were reasons why I didn't and now I realize that, at the time, they were good reasons to me, but I missed out a lot involving my family and you." Roxie felt horrible. She had been so mad that her mom had tricked her into coming home that she had put Devon's mom out of her mind. Expecting to see Lilly Baxter coming through the door was something that she would have to get over; Lilly was gone forever.

"It's all right. I'm sorry I exploded on you for everything."

"No I deserved it." Roxie sniffed and then realized how close she was to Devon. She stepped back to put some distance between them, but Devon had other ideas and tightened his arms around her.

"Just for a minute let me hold you and think back to a better time and place." Roxie relaxed and relished the feelings coming over her. She thought she would never be back in Devon's life again. After several minutes Devon finally released her and surprised her by saying, "I will still go along with your plan about your mother as long as it doesn't go on for more than a few days. Let's just to make her sweat a little bit."

Roxie was stunned for a second and then asked, "Why?"

He looked at her sheepishly and stated simply, "Frankly it will be fun to be a part of a team like we used to be back when we were kids."

She started laughing, remembering all the pranks they had pulled as kids and all the trouble they had gotten into with their parents. "All right you convinced me."

Chapter 5

"Now that all that is out of the way, you need to tell me why you couldn't come back after eleven years and what you've been doing in all that time," Devon said. Not knowing what she was doing for all these years had truly been eating him up inside.

Roxie realized then that Devon had truly cared for her. If he hadn't cared, it wouldn't have bothered him so much that he didn't know what or where she had been in the last few years. She also knew that the quickest way to get him to run the other way would be tell him her feelings had never changed. She decided it was time to quit running from her past and lay it all on the line once and for all.

"Sit down, Dev. I have a feeling you might want to after what I tell you."

He looked at her quizzically, but sat down on the sofa and she came around the table and sat at the other end.

"Please don't say anything until I finish," she said. She didn't continue until she saw him nod in agreement. "The reason I left was because I didn't know if you loved me or not. I've loved you for so long. Looking back I realized I was being selfish wanting to keep you to myself, not knowing if you returned my feelings. Oh I know you loved me, but I didn't know what kind of love you felt for me. I was worried that you loved me as a friend and not as a lover. I guess I left to test that love and when you didn't come for me I couldn't bare coming back and watching you live your life without me."

At that moment Devon couldn't have spoken if he had wanted to. It was just like Roxie to be as blunt as possible and this time he was grateful because he would finally get to tell her how he felt now that he knew her true feelings. He opened his mouth to try to form the words to tell her how he felt, but she raised her hand.

"Please let me finish. Don't say anything just because you feel pity for me. We have been friends for too long to lie to each other. I broke the trust eleven years ago when I left and tried to force your hand in telling me what I wanted to hear. We both needed to grow up at that time.

"I was mad when I had found out mom lied to me, but now I realize it was also relief that I would finally have my chance to let you know how I felt after all these years. Please, I don't want any declarations or set downs tonight; I just want to relish being home and being with a best friend that I have missed for far too long. Will you agree to think over everything I've said and when it has all sunk in then we will both speak of any feelings we have and then decide what to do?"

Roxie waited with bated breath more nervous than her first board meeting six years ago, but she lifted her chin and stared Devon in the eye until he finally spoke.

"I don't agree," he said breaking through the silence. "I've been wanting to tell you something for a lot of years, but I will respect your request only because I don't want you thinking that what you said influences what I have to tell you. So for now we'll leave it and change the subject slightly."

Thank god. She didn't know what she would have done if he had told her to leave the house or returned her feelings out of pity. "What does slightly mean, exactly?"

"Where have you been? Please the truth, no bull."

Roxie debated whether to tell Devon the whole truth and decided that if she was going to start out on the right foot for the future (as she was hoping would happen) she needed to be as honest as possible now.

Devon watched the emotions on Roxie's face and waited. He knew she was deciding what to tell him and could only hope she would trust him enough with the entire story.

"I've been a lot of places, traveled overseas for a while and truly had a blast. Worked odd jobs to make ends meet, met a wide range of people.

"Is that all you've done this entire time? I mean what kind of life is that to lead for any number of years, let alone eleven?" He was exasperated with her, anything could've of happened to her any number of times. It made his skin crawl just to think about it.

"Are you done or do you want to hear the rest of the story?" Amusement shone in her eyes as she looked at him and she was struggling not to smile, but figured that might be unwise considering she could tell he truly was upset about what might have happened to her during her travels.

"Fine." He bit off the reply. "Tell me the rest."

"Basically I only traveled a few years before I settled down in New York. I got a couple of different jobs to pay for rent and to buy a used computer. After I had enough money for the computer, I saved enough money for online college courses in Business Administration." She waited for Devon's reaction to hearing she had attended classes, even if it was over the internet, but he seemed patient enough to let her continue so, twisting her hands in her lap nervously, she continued with the hardest part of the story.

"I was one of the few lucky people that was selected in an intern position a few years after I had started taking my courses. The intern position was with a prestigious investment firm. I worked my butt off for an additional year during the program. It paid off because I was eventually asked to join the firm on a permanent basis. Since then I have climbed the corporate ladder until I became a senior partner in the firm, which is unheard of in the industry for someone my age, but I feel I've truly worked hard for my position and I love what I've done with my life."

Roxie took a breath and looked Devon in the eye. She was rocked by the anger she saw in his stormy green eyes, but she also saw respect and admiration and could only hope that the latter won out.

"Say something, I truly want to be as honest with you as possible."

Devon had to take a minute to collect his thoughts, he was just glad he hadn't offered to buy her new clothes. Talk about looking like a fool. Which brought up a question of why she looked like she was wearing hand-me-downs and came to town on the bus. Was she lying after all? "Why arrive on the bus? And your clothes... I don't understand."

She had momentarily forgot about those details. Oh well time to come clean.

"I wanted to come home and settle a few days before telling anybody about my lifestyle. Knowing small towns, if I had arrived in my BMW and designer clothes I definitely would have gotten some looks. I mean, having left here straight out of high school and with nobody hearing from me except for my parents, I would be the center of a nasty rumor in no time. Everyone would be saying that I only slept with rich men and was somebody's sugar baby. Also I guess in a way I felt ashamed to tell my parents how well I have done because I have never told them the truth beyond that I am still traveling and doing odd jobs for money."

"Exactly how well are you doing at the investment firm? You know, money wise, if you don't mind me asking."

"I'm a millionaire several times over. I could've easily taken the company jet straight here instead of flying commercial," Roxie said. She kept her eyes downcast, afraid to look up at Devon and see his reaction.

Devon found himself taking a deep breath before he said anything else. Damn, she was rich and could probably buy ranches like his with no problem. She'd never even miss the money. It wasn't like Devon was poor by any means, but he always believed that when Roxie came home she would actually *need him* for something. This changed things, but maybe she would still come home to stay. After all, if she had all that money maybe she wouldn't mind giving her job up for a life with him on the ranch. She had accomplished more in a few short years that very few people realized in a lifetime.

"Say something Devon. You're scaring me."

"I don't know what to say; you obviously have everything you could want."

"Not everything," Roxie whispered. She said it so quietly that for a moment Devon wasn't even sure she had said it, but it gave him hope.

"Look, I guess I wanted you to actually need us back home for something, but you're you Roxie; you've always been strong and determined. Heck, I'm proud you made something of yourself and didn't waste the potential everybody saw in you when we were kids." The next thing Devon knew, Roxie flung her body into his lap and kissed him soundly on the mouth. She hugged him fiercely.

"What's this all about?" he asked bewildered by her reaction.

"Thank you, Dev. You didn't have to be so understanding about all of this."

"We were best friends once. We used to be able to tell each other anything. Why did you think that would ever change? I still consider you by best friend, Roxie. If you believe nothing else always believe that."

Roxie's eyes started filling with tears and she slid off Devon's lap and went to sit back in her chair across from him.

Before she could say anything else and tell him how happy she was at the moment, he looked at her and stated, "Look it's late and we both need sleep, you especially since you've been traveling. Why don't we go to bed, sleep on everything and talk in the morning; what do you say?"

Roxie could only nod her head. She truly was exhausted and relieved to have one hurdle out of the way.

Chapter 6

The next morning over breakfast Devon announced he was going over to her parent's house to visit with them for a while.

"Devon, I want to drop my whole plan of my so-called 'revenge' against my mom. I know she only wanted me home."

"Are you sure?"

"Yes." She was positive, but now she also nervous; she hadn't seen her parents in so long and she didn't want to see the disappointment in their eyes from not having come home sooner.

"Well, why don't we still give them a surprise? It doesn't have to be prolonged. We'll go over in my pickup. It's got dark tinting on the windows and they won't be able to see you if you're in the cab. When I get in the house, I'll talk to your parents. I'll still play along like I've met someone new, then I will signal for you, giving them the best surprise they've had all year."

"If that's what you think we should do, okay I'm with you."

"Look, after the past week everybody could use a good laugh and I especially would like to see the joy on your parents' faces when you come through the door," Devon said simply.

"All right when do we leave? I'm anxious to see them after so long."

"Since it's already nine o'clock, I don't see why we can't head over there now." He was really wanting to be selfish and keep her to himself for the rest of the day, but her parents deserved to know she was home, however temporary.

"Okay then it's settled, just let me go get changed." She was still wearing her pajamas and robe.

Twenty minutes later they were headed out to her parents' ranch and each second that passed her stomach turned into so many knots that she felt she was going to be sick. When they finally arrived at the ranch, Devon went to house like planned only to be told by Lou's foreman that Lou and Milly had started out early for the city for Lou's checkup and a day of shopping.

He walked back to the truck trying to hide his smile, but didn't quite manage it because it looked like he was going to get his wish after all. He would get to spend the day with Roxie alone at the house. He slid into the cab of the pickup and looked into Roxie's anxious eyes. He realized how torn up she truly was and sobered immediately. Telling her the news, he watched her visibly relax.

He started the truck and, in seconds, they were well on their way back to his house. When they arrived back, they both walked in and awkwardly stood a few feet from each other, neither one had said a word on the drive from Roxie's parent's house.

Trying to ease the tension a little, Devon asked, "Well is there anything special you want to do on your first day back? We could go horseback riding, or go into town and eat lunch. Whatever you choose that's what we'll do. I'll just let my foreman know that I'm going to be unavailable today." Devon hoped she wanted to just hang around the house and spend time with him. He knew that once her parents came home they would monopolize the majority of her time in Peace before she left to go back to New York.

For the entire time Devon had been talking, Roxie had been wandering around the living room and the tension slowly eased from her body. 'Something special', he'd said. Oh yeah she wanted to do something special all right, but she didn't know if what she planned would be the smartest move on her part or not, but she had denied herself for far too long.

She started smiling and didn't realize it until she noticed the expression on Devon's face. His soulful eyes were looking back at her suspiciously and oddly hopeful. Did he know that all she wanted to do today was spend it with him and finally have the first kiss that they never got to experience all those years ago? Well, okay technically it would be the second kiss, but a person couldn't count the kiss at the bus stop; it was just a joyous kiss between two old friends. Yeah right, it had knocked her socks off. Oh well, this time she wanted to do it right.

Devon was holding his breath because he wasn't sure what to expect from Roxie. He never knew what to expect from her and it always frustrated the hell out of him. He watched her warily as she approached him with that darn smile on her face and it took everything in him not to pick her up and take her straight to his bedroom or hers... whichever one they came to first. In fact he didn't much care if they even made it to the bedroom.

"What I want is this, Cowboy." She kissed him with everything she had and then some.

YES! That was all Devon could think of. Then he didn't have time for any more thoughts as Roxie started running her hands over his body. He had too many clothes on and his brain couldn't function to take them off.

Breathing heavily, Roxie pulled her mouth from his and asked hoarsely, "Here or the bedroom? Frankly I hope you don't say the bedroom because I doubt we'll make it that far, but it might be fun to try." She knew she was coming on strong, but they had known each other for a long time and she wouldn't be able to hide anything from him anyway.

He didn't disappoint her. He never stated his preference in words; he simply looked her up and down in a way that sent a shiver up her body. Then he proceeded to take her clothes off. They didn't bother with the couch, but instead found themselves on the living room floor rug.

"Ah, Roxie. I've wanted you for so long. I can't believe you're actually here."

Not the declaration of love she was looking for, but what could she expect? They were about to have sex on his living room floor.

"I would have come home sooner if I'd known this was the welcome I'd get. She buried her face in his neck and inhaled. She loved the cologne he always wore.

They still had on several articles of clothing, only managing to remove their shirts and shoes. When Devon looked up at her and started removing her jeans, he heard a noise that sounded like someone clearing their throat. They weren't alone. Devon and Roxie tensed at the same time.

Devon raised his head to look around the side of the couch since they were in front of it on the floor.

What he saw was not welcoming. Lou and Milly Lancaster were standing in the doorway, shock written all over their faces. He could well understand. For the last eleven years the only thoughts he had was about their daughter; he knew they knew he was in love with Roxie. Then he realized they couldn't see Roxie because of the couch and he couldn't help but start to laugh. He didn't stop until Roxie punched him in the ribs and asked him who was around the couch.

By this time her parents had backed out of the living room, mumbling about being in the kitchen.

"It's your parents, Honey." He looked down at her and the expression was priceless.

Her eyes were round with shock and she kept opening her mouth to say something, but it seemed she couldn't say a word. Finally she asked, "My parents? But they went to the city; are you sure?"

Laughing harder at this point Devon assured her that he was sure.

"This is not funny, Dev. How am I going to explain this? First I come home and don't even let them know I'm in town. Then I decide to stay here with you instead of them and now they catch me almost having sex with you on your living room floor." By this point Roxie was extremely agitated.

"Honey, that's why I'm laughing. They couldn't see you for the couch, so you can still save face by going and straightening up and staying in your room. We can still keep them in the dark about you being here if you want. My personal life isn't any of their business. I can keep quiet about who was in here if that's what you want." Devon didn't like to lie to her parents, but he would do anything at this point to keep her here with him.

Roxie looked with disbelief at Devon, realizing how much she truly loved him, but she drew the line at him lying to her parents for her. No, she needed to end this and face her parents once and for all, no matter how embarrassing this would be for her. She looked up at him. He was still on top of her on the floor.

"I appreciate that you would do that for me Devon, but I don't want you to lie for me. I'll handle this situation; I need to finally face my parents. If you'll go stall them then I can go upstairs real quick and get straightened up before I see them. Will you do that for me?"

Devon let out a sigh of relief. He was hoping she would handle this; he didn't relish lying to them.

"Yes, I'll go stall them for you and then I'll be there for you when you explain everything, but don't forget that you also need an explanation from your mother for her lying to you to get you to come home." As he was saying this he rolled off Roxie and helped her to her feet and they both started getting redressed.

"I won't forget. Thanks Dev. I'll see you in a minute, okay?"

"Okay." He watched her walk out of the living room and turn back right towards the staircase. He knew her parents wouldn't spot her because he doubted they would leave the kitchen until he showed his face to them. He sighed and looked down at his clothes to make sure that everything looked in order. There was nothing like parents walking in to kill the mood. Oh well, he better get to the kitchen and find out why her parents weren't in the city like he had been told.

When he walked in he could tell immediately that they were more embarrassed by the situation than he was, but he also knew that once Lou realized it was his daughter he had almost seen naked all friendliness would leave Lou's face in an instant. Devon needed to play this right. Hopefully Roxie's parents would be too astonished to see their daughter and would forget all about attacking him for his morals; yeah right, like that was going to happen.

Lou was the first to speak, albeit gruffly, "Son, I'm sorry we walked in on you and your friend. We tried knocking on your front door, but you didn't answer and your truck was in the drive. When we got home our foreman said you had stopped by to see us. He seemed to think it was important, so we came over immediately. Frankly we were kind of hoping you had word of Roxie."

"Why would you think I would have word of Roxie?" Devon asked, even though he knew the answer. He watched Milly move her hands nervously in her lap.

"Go ahead Milly, answer him."

"I just wanted her to come home for once and I used the knowledge that she loves you to do it, so I told her that you were in critical condition at the hospital and that you would need a miracle to come out of it. I know it was terrible to tell her that, especially after your mother was killed in the very accident I told Roxie you were involved in. I guess nothing will make her come home... not even her love for you. I just don't understand it; you two belong together. She should be with us, her family, not traveling all over the world. Do you forgive me, Devon? You're like my own son. I wouldn't deliberately hurt you for anything. I can see you've moved on, if what we walked in on earlier is any indication, so please tell your lady friend she can come out of whatever room you've put her in... unless she's too embarrassed." Milly said all this in a rush, hoping Devon would forgive her. She had witnessed how much it had hurt Devon to be without Roxie all these years. If Devon was finally over Roxie, then they'd have to accept it and move on.. She looked up and realized that Devon was smiling. She looked over at her husband, but he just shrugged and looked back at Devon.

By now Devon's shoulders were shaking with laughter and he had no doubt that Roxie was outside the kitchen door and had been listening in while her mother gave her speech.

"I'm sure she's going to be embarrassed, but she said she wants to see you both," Devon said.

Lou looked at his wife and could tell she was getting angry with Devon for laughing because she couldn't find anything funny about the situation, so he asked, "What's so funny? You're keeping us in the dark about something aren't you?"

Devon looked at Roxie's parents while he spoke. He truly wanted to see the expression on their faces when Roxie came through the kitchen door.

"Come on Honey, quit eavesdropping through the door and get in here and face the music." He heard the door open behind him and watched the shock register on their faces. Devon had to hide a smile as Roxie said, "Hi Mom, Dad. Long time no see."

Milly fainted. Lou looked especially angry. Devon wiped the grin off his face.

Chapter 7

"Mom? Mom! Oh my gosh I didn't mean to make her faint!" Roxie ran around the kitchen table to her mother's side, but immediately shrank away from the anger in her father's eyes. "Dad?" she said warily.

"Leave us, both of you, while I bring Milly around. Then we'll talk." Lou didn't bother to look at either one of them as he spoke.

"But Dad let me help." Roxie rose from her position beside her mom looking down at her father's face with disbelief.

"You haven't bothered about your mother's feelings for eleven years, now leave." Lou's face was getting redder by the second and she was afraid he was holding his breath to keep what composure he had.

Devon realized instantly that Roxie's refusal to come home had caused a serious problem between her and her parents that would take a great deal of time to heal. He turned to Roxie and placed his hand on her arm to lead her from the kitchen. She was so stunned she didn't protest.

He took her to the living room and pushed her onto an overstuffed chair opposite the couch that overlooked the front yard. She didn't bother moving for several minutes; she just sat there and stared out the window while silent tears fell from her Honey colored eyes that he loved so well. As much as he hated to see her hurting, he also understood the hurt that her parents must be feeling.

"I didn't realize what I had done, until now." Roxie had whispered the words so low that Devon barely heard her, but he heard her next statement clearly. "You were right last night Devon; I am extremely selfish."

He didn't contradict her.

Devon had concentrated so much on having her back that he hadn't truly analyzed his feelings. Suddenly he realized he could be just as angry as her father seemed to be a few minutes ago in the kitchen. Anger would be so easy, but then he looked at Roxie's face and knew that she was just as tormented as a person could get. She had caused the people she loved the most so much pain. It had been the worst and best week of his life so far. He just felt so tired all of a sudden.

At that moment Milly and Lou walked in and both looked at their daughter they hadn't seen in so long. Milly was visibly excited, but trying not to rush across the room to her daughter. Devon figured Lou had spoken to her about taking it slow. Lou still had a red flush to his face from his anger, but his eyes betrayed his true feelings... that he was just as eager to greet his daughter. It seemed everybody in the room was holding their breath for somebody to take the first move.

In the next instant Devon wasn't sure what had happened. All he saw was Milly and Roxie start crying again and cross the room at the same time to hug, when his living room window shattered and he heard the single shot of a gun.

"HIT THE FLOOR!" Devon yelled. Yeah, like he really needed to tell them all to hit the floor; it wasn't likely any of them would keep standing after having all been missed by a bullet.

While everybody was still on the floor, Devon belly crawled to the edge of the bay window and looked out. Shock filled his face when he surprisingly saw his foreman running towards the front door with his hunting rifle.

Todd Wicks, Devon's foreman, ran into the house and straight into the living room looking as ashamed as a human being can get and started to shakily ask, "Is anybody ..."

Devon was so furious that he didn't recall crossing the room and picking the man up by his throat and slamming him into the wall. "What the heck did you think you were doing? You are very lucky that the bullet missed everybody in this house or your butt would already be sitting in a county jail cell."

By now Roxie and her parents had gotten up from the floor and Roxie rushed to Devon's side. "Devon let him go and let him explain before you completely choke him to death and he can't tell you anything." She had her hands on Devon's right forearm pulling with all her strength and couldn't break his hold.

Lou stepped over to where Devon was standing. "Let him go son. Let him explain."

One by one the muscles in Devon's face relaxed and he released his hold on Todd. "Explain, and it better be the best darned reason in your life or you lose the job you've had with me for five years."

"I'm sorry Mr. Baxter," Todd rasped, he could feel his throat swelling up from the bruising hands of Baxter. "Rattlesnake in the yard. I missed and hit a rock. The next thing I heard was the glass breaking and yelling. I wouldn't for all the world hurt you or your friends." Todd wasn't sure, but he hoped Devon would show leniency towards him. He didn't relish going to jail or having Devon's hands back on his throat.

"All right, get out of my sight and stay away. I realize that it was an accident, but I'm still royally pissed that you almost shot one of us because of your carelessness."

"Yes sir, boss... and again I'm sorry." Todd turned and ran from the house as fast as he could. He stayed out of sight for almost a week.

"Devon, it was an accident, try not to be so hard on him."

"Shoot, Roxie I don't care if it was accident. I can't afford for a grown man employed on this ranch to be so careless. I just lost my mother to an accident; I don't want to lose anybody else I care about and I care about all of you. Now if you will excuse me I need to cool off. Why don't you use my office to catch up with your parents?" With that Devon turned and left the house for several hours.

A little awkwardly, Roxie and her parents made their way to the office, nobody saying anything until they made it into the room and shut the door. The emotional upheaval from earlier seemed completely gone and a strange calm came over the small group.

Roxie decided that she needed to make this right with her parents and she knew it would take a while for them to forgive her for the choices she had made in her life.

"Mom, Dad, I'm sorry that I stayed away for so long. I'm even sorrier that it took you, Mom, to lie to me about Devon for me to come home. I'm so ashamed and hope you can forgive me someday for my selfishness." Roxie looked anxiously from one parent to the other; she knew her father was extremely angry with her and hoped that they could mend their fences.

"Roxie, we knew why you stayed away all these years and I also need to apologize to you for lying to you about Devon. I just felt that it was time you came home and Devon was the only option I had left to see the daughter we had raised. Your father warned me about my plan and wanted no part of it, so please don't blame him for any of this," Milly said.

"Oh Mom you have nothing to apologize for. Dad please stop glowering at me, I feel horrible for how I've treated you both," Roxie said.

Lou face softened ever so much and he cleared his throat. "I'm sorry, Roxie. I'm glad you've finally come home, but I don't think you know why I'm so angry with you."

"I just figured you were angry at me for being gone so long," Roxie said feeling a bit confused.

"That's what I thought. You don't know why I'm angry," Lou said a little on the sarcastic side.

"Then tell me, Dad." The group had made itself comfortable in the office. Roxie had taken up the single chair in the room, while her parents rested on the loveseat adjacent to her position. Her father was sitting rigidly with every muscle tensed in his face.

"All right, I'll tell you. I'm upset because after eleven years it takes your mother calling you and having to lie about Devon to get you to come home. Because after eleven years when you do come home, because of DEVON not US, we find you here in Devon's house, not our house. You didn't even bother to call us first when you reached town; you obviously contacted Devon first, not to mention the compromising situation we walked into earlier today in Devon's living room." Lou's anger earlier was nothing compared to the anger she saw in her dad's eyes at that moment.

Roxie realized how serious her dad was because that was truly the most words to come out of her dad's mouth at one time and her mom hadn't said a word in the entire speech. Roxie knew that she needed to be as honest with her parents as she had been with Devon last night to hopefully ease their minds about her and her past and how she had truly come to be at Devon's house and not theirs when she had gotten to town.

She told them everything from the time that mom had called her to the time that they had show up at Devon's house and walked in on them; she felt it prudent for everybody to actually exclude the conversation with Devon the previous night, especially about the plan to get back at her mom for lying to her and her actions between Devon and herself that they had walked in on. She only hoped that her parents wouldn't push that particular issue. They didn't.

The entire time she was talking she saw her dad visibly starting to relax.

"That's it." She held her hands out in front of her and watched as her parents looked at each other before speaking.

"Although we are still upset, we understand to a point and can only hope that you are home to stay for a while to catch up. As much as we would like to have you home for good, we also realize that you're grown and will live where you choose," Lou paused and then asked the one she had been waiting for. "Roxie just exactly what have you been doing for the last eleven years?"

Roxie then again told them the complete truth hoping that they wouldn't find too much fault with her for withholding from them once again. It was a different set of emotions crossing her parents' faces as she told them about her life and what she had accomplished with it. Their emotions ranged from surprise and then pride as they realized the daughter they raised had truly come out stronger than most people who had left home at the tender age of eighteen.

"Well we are proud of you for what you have accomplished with your life; we just wish we could have been a part of it," Milly finally said after a few minutes of silence.

"I know. I just hope you both forgive me for my actions. I promise I won't leave home again without coming home again for visits." Roxie purposely left the statement open so that her parents wouldn't believe she had come home permanently. She still didn't know what her future was with Devon. "We can accept that for now, but don't think we won't try to keep you home for as long as possible," Milly impishly replied.

"Well, now that we've talked things out, we expect you to collect your things and stay with us. We don't want to treat you like a child, but I especially can't abide my daughter living with a man, however temporary, and we hope you'll come home as a courtesy to us. We haven't seen you in so long and hope we could catch up." Lou said not going to be swayed on this point.

"Of course Dad, but let's compromise. I was hoping that Devon could bring me home in a little while. I'd like the chance to explain everything to him before taking off to your place," Roxie said, hoping they would understand.

"All right, but if you're not home by nightfall I'll come back for you." Lou looked uncompromising on this issue and Roxie knew that she wouldn't persuade her father otherwise.

"Deal."

Soon after both her parents left she went to her temporary room to collect her things and bring them back to the foyer so that they would be ready when Devon got back to the house.

Meanwhile, the foreman Todd Wicks was making a phone call to his other boss.

"I missed." Wicks was sweating profusely. Devon scared the hell out of him, but this guy that had hired him for this particular job was nobody to mess with and he soon found himself between a rock and a hard spot.

"I should have known that to hire a hick Cowboy like you to do the job would fall through. Did anybody suspect anything?" The voice on the phone was so cold that it sent a shiver down Wicks' spine.

"No sir; I gave a plausible excuse, even though Baxter was mighty pissed with me at the moment." Wicks explained about the rattlesnake story and then trailed off because he realized this man didn't care as long as the job was done and it wasn't.

"I'll get him next time, sir."

"You had better because if you don't, you won't have a third chance. Don't think for one minute I don't have others in my employ that will take care of you if the job's not done to my satisfaction."

"I ..." Wicks started to respond, but before he could sputter another word the line had already went dead and he didn't know if the dead silence on the other end was in fact an omen to his own demise.

Chapter 8

The next day, Roxie slept in for the first time in a long time and felt like she had been transported back to her childhood. She slowly opened her eyes and simply took in the room around her. Her parents had kept the room exactly the same since she had left. It seemed surreal. There were trophies and ribbons for barrel racing competitions, posters from her favorite movies at the time and a picture on the bedside table of her favorite horse Belles. She suddenly needed to find out about her horse, even though Belles had been four years old when Roxie had left, she would only be fifteen now.

Before she could give anything else a second thought, Roxie threw back the covers of her full size bed. She really missed her king size bed in her apartment, not so much her apartment, but definitely her bed. As she ran from her room down the hall to the kitchen she could hear her parents. It was just like old times and it was hard to imagine she was actually here.

As she burst through the kitchen door, Milly looked up from the bacon that was sizzling on the griddle and was momentarily surprised to see her daughter standing there. She knew she was being foolish, but it was still hard to believe that her daughter had finally come home.

"Want some breakfast?"

"Love some. Um, Dad?" Roxie was glad to see that the anger from yesterday in her father's eyes was now gone. She didn't think she could handle a second day with him angry with her.

"Yeah?"

"Belles?"

"In her stall. Why?" Lou watched as his daughter visibly relaxed and then ran out the backdoor like there was a fire behind her. He started chuckling; he knew that would get her out the door. That girl of his always had been a sucker for her horse.

Milly looked around when she heard the back door slam shut and went to the door and hollered, "What about breakfast?" She saw Roxie give a little wave without turning around and realized that was the only acknowledgement she would get. Roxie was just like her daddy. They had both always been horse crazy and Roxie was especially crazy about that buckskin horse of hers. That's another reason it had always surprised her that Roxie had stayed away from the ranch; Milly knew how much she truly loved the country.

"Are you going to stand there all day or serve up breakfast? She'll be back in a little while." However reassuring he meant to be, Lou was still insecure and was couldn't help be afraid his daughter would leave again, but wasn't going to show his wife that; he needed to be the strong one for her.

"Your legs aren't broke, old man. I'll stare out the door all I want." Having said this Milly turned back into the kitchen to fix her husband a plate, just like the old codger knew she would. She smiled when she knew he couldn't see her. After thirty years she would still do anything for the man, even when there were times when he could make her blood boil. She also knew how worried he was that his daughter would pick up and leave again. Well they would just need to make a plan to get their daughter married and settled before the year was out so that Roxie wouldn't leave again.

Roxie raced into the barn still in her pajamas. In her excitement, she never bothered to change; she didn't care, she just wanted to see her beloved horse. It was a beautiful, but chilly morning. However, the sunlight was bright on her eyes, so when she entered the barn she stopped to let her eyes adjust to the dimness before walking down the familiar aisle. There were some of the best quarter horses in the state in her parents' horse barn, but Roxie was only concentrating on a certain buckskin horse. Belles had a dark golden color body with black that ran up her legs to her knees and hocks and a coal black main and tail.

Finally, on the left side of the barn was Belles' stall. It was marked by a nameplate that was still shiny with black engraved letters to showcase her horse's name just like every horse had in the barn. "Belles?" Roxie peered into the stall and was instantly met by her mare. "Ah, there you are girl. I missed you."

Roxie opened the stall gate and stood as close to her horse as she could. She stroked her soft neck and spoke softly to her.

"It's been a long time since you've seen each other."

Roxie spun on her heel to come face to face with Devon.

"What are you doing here?" she asked. They had talked the evening before and they had both agreed she was going to spend today at her parents' house. They would start spending time together the next day or so.

"Well, I'm not here to see you, but your dad." He watched amused as she tried not to look offended, but decided against it.

"Well he's in the house. If you hurry you can still catch breakfast." Roxie was feeling decidedly uncomfortable standing in her horse's stall wearing only her pajamas.

"I figured, but when I was driving up the lane your mad dash to the barn caught my eye and I couldn't resist seeing the reunion. Hope you don't mind the intrusion?" He realized then she was embarrassed from the color staining her cheeks. "Why the blush? You can't possibly be embarrassed in front of me? I mean especially after yesterday." Women! He would never understand them.

Men! They were so dense sometimes. I mean didn't he know that was why she was embarrassed, especially after yesterday. Ignoring him, Roxie said goodbye to Belles and closed the stall door.

"Come on then," she beckoned. She left the barn expecting him to follow. He didn't disappoint.

He knew she was avoiding the issue. Oh well he would let it go for now. He really did need to talk to her father.

Back in the Lancaster kitchen, Devon sat at the table opposite Lou and watched as Roxie told her parents she was going to take a shower and change. While he watched her leave the room, she looked back at him making sure her parents weren't looking and stuck her tongue out at him like she used to do when they were kids and she was annoyed with him.

Roxie didn't know what had come over her, but there she was like a kid again sticking her tongue out at Devon and then a slow smile came to his mouth and his green eyes looked at her with smoldering intent and if she didn't already love him that look would have done it in for her right then and there. Trying to keep from fanning herself as she left the kitchen, Roxie sighed and darted for the stairs. She knew that a blush had come back to her cheeks and she prayed her parents had missed the byplay between them.

They didn't and hid their smiles in their coffee cups acting none the wiser.

Milly had gotten up and had already fixed Devon a plate. She set it in front of him with quiet determination. Since his mother was no longer around, she would look out for him. After all, he was already like a son to her and his mother had been one of her closest friends. "Thanks Mrs. Lancaster"

"When are you going to finally call me Milly? Mrs. Lancaster sounds so old."

Devon just smiled at her with that crooked grin of his. They had this conversation every time he came over for something to eat.

Since Lou hadn't spoken a word to him since he had come into the house, he could only hope that yesterday's anger at catching him and Roxie together would pass. Since he had permanent future plans to discuss with her as soon as they were able, but at the moment he had another problem.

"Lou, I was riding boundary fences this morning and our north border fence has been cut and tracks showed cattle crossing over to your place." Devon had really only come over here as a formality to a neighbor; he didn't like to ride on other people's property without letting them know first. Misunderstandings had happened on a lot less.

"No problem Devon. Do you need help gathering your cattle? How many are missing?"

"No I can get my guys to do it. I've got about ten head gone along with one of my best bulls."

"You're sure the wire was cut?"

"Yeah, I don't know why anybody would bother. My boys know if they cut a fence that there better be a damn good reason. I've asked all of them if they had a reason for the cut, but nobody claims to have been in the north section in the last few days."

"Strange. Let me know when you find your cattle and if you do need any additional help."

"Will do. Mrs. Lancaster, thank you again for a wonderful breakfast. Will you let Roxie know I'll call her tomorrow or the next day? You know, give her time to get settled."

"Of course… and Devon we promise not to monopolize her time so that you can spend as much time with her as you can." Milly wanted to let him know that he had their blessing for the relationship she hoped would develop between her daughter and this man.

"Thank you both." Devon left through the way he had come, the back door. It came as no surprise Lou and Milly supported him, they alone knew how much he had truly pined for Roxie all these years. He shook the thoughts from his head. It was time to round up some missing cattle.

Four hours later Devon was swearing a blue streak and wondering how, on such a beautiful day, he had landed on his butt in a thorn bush. He had chosen his best horse, a grey named Blue that had impeccable cutting bloodlines, to gather the cattle only to find his self bucked off, and the worst wasn't over yet.

He heard the laughter before he saw her and closed his eyes and prayed it was his imagination, but as he got up from the ground, wincing from the thorns imbedded in his skin and pulling at his clothes, he noticed her standing a few yards away on her mare, Belles.

"I thought Cowboys could ride better than that. I mean I know your riding skills, but I thought it took more than a few hops to throw you from a horse." Roxie wanted to let loose with a full belly laugh, but one look at Devon made her think better of it so she settled for a little bit of laughter at his expense.

Devon cut his eyes towards her and looked ferocious enough to hurt anything in his path and then ruined everything by grabbing the back of his pants and lifting one leg and then another trying to pull the thorns loose. It was a comical sight to see such a tough man show this moment of weakness.

Roxie couldn't help it; she started laughing until she was crying. Finally she slid from her horse onto the ground and kept laughing until he thought he was going to have to choke her to get her to shut up. "It's not that funny," Devon snapped

All she did was hold up a hand to wipe the tears from her eyes. He just rolled his eyes.

"If you can finish laughing long enough, maybe a little help wouldn't be too much trouble." He wasn't angry anymore, but darn did these thorns hurt like hell and, to top everything off, his horse was most likely back at his barn by now.

"I'm sorry," Roxie said breathlessly from her spot on the ground. "Come over here and turn around so that I can get the thorns out."

"Why don't you come over here? If I move anymore they will become permanently embedded." He wasn't about to make an even bigger fool of himself again. Lord, she was beautiful with her long blond hair braided to keep it out of her face and those Honey colored eyes that were even more appealing when they were lit up with amusement.

"All right." Finally, with all the laughs out of the way, Roxie felt better than she had in ages; she'd truly forgotten what it was like when they were kids and used to laugh all the time together. "Let me look at your butt."

"Not a problem darling. With or without clothes?" he smirked.

"Without if you don't mind," Roxie said, just as amused. Two could play at this game. She almost started laughing again when she saw the surprise in his eyes and then all laughter stopped as a challenging light came to his eyes and he started reaching for his belt buckle. Next thing she knew he pulled his pants down around his ankles. Thank god he had on boxers. She didn't know what she would have done if he had been completely naked. She probably would have jumped him, but then he would have landed on his rear end again and cursed her because the thorns were still in his butt.

He watched her with appreciation because Roxie didn't so much as blink an eye, but did stand completely still for a few moments and then started around him, dropping to the ground behind him. He waited for her to start pulling the thorns and kept waiting. Finally he looked over his shoulder and saw Roxie's eyes fixated on his butt and he couldn't help but laugh at her. "What's wrong darling, never seen a butt before?"

Roxie just rolled her expressive eyes at him and proceeded to pull out the thorns and not gently, he had to keep from wincing a few times. "Of course, but I can't help from noticing what nice butt you really have."

"Well at least there's something about me you find irresistible."

"Oh please, you give a man a compliment and it goes straight to his head."

After all the thorns were taken care of, and Devon had pulled his jeans back up Roxie was back to wondering about his cattle.

"So dad said you had some fence trouble and your cattle were over here. Did you find them?"

All of a sudden Devon was angry all over again, but not at her, it was the situation.

"No not yet."

"Well how many are gone? I'll help you look."

"About ten head. Among that number was one of my best bulls."

"Okay well you can ride double with me and we'll go get you another horse and come back and find them."

"I appreciate it and I'll take you up on the ride, but we're not coming back."

Roxie looked at him with a puzzled expression on her face and realized he was really angry about something, but knew it wasn't directed towards her.

"Why not, Dev?"

"Because I need to get home and call the sheriff and talk to your dad."

"I still don't understand."

By now he was looking back towards the back section where the gate was. His eyes were fixated on fresh tire tracks from a truck and trailer. "My cattle have been stolen from your dad's pasture."

Chapter 9

"What do you mean they've been stolen?"

Although he was listening to Roxie, Devon had an uneasy feeling that they were being watched. He turned in a slow circle scanning the horizon for any places that a person could hide and watch undisturbed; unfortunately there were many such places. They needed to get out of there and fast. "We need to go now."

Roxie was starting to think that maybe Devon had hit the ground harder than she thought. "Devon? Are you feeling all right? Maybe..." She never got to finish her sentence before a shot rang out and the bullet hit the ground right between their feet.

"Get to Belles, quick!" Devon shouted. "Move now."

Thankfully Belles wasn't gun shy. She was still standing in the same spot that Roxie had left her, but feeling the tension in the air, the horse was becoming nervous. As Roxie and Devon raced to the horse she became panicked and started sidestepping.

"Talk to her Roxie; she's our only way out of here."

Finally, after crooning to the horse and getting her calm enough, they both got mounted and turned her towards Devon's place, racing her at a breakneck pace. There hadn't been another shot so neither one of them knew if the shooter only meant it as a warning shot or, given the amount of time that they had heard the shot and gotten to the horse, the shooter simply hadn't had time to take another shot at them.

Behind a massive oak tree Devon's foreman was badly shaking; he couldn't believe he had missed. He rarely missed when he shot at a target. The problem was he had never tried to kill another human being before and Roxie Lancaster showing up had surprised him also. He'd watched the by play between the two for a while before making his shot, but in the end had failed a second time. Crap, crap, crap... He was told he only had the one chance left and he had screwed that up. Hands shaking, Todd pulled his cigarettes and lighter from his breast pocket and lit one up to calm his nerves. He just wished at that moment for a shot of whiskey. Even though the payment on the job was good, it wouldn't do him any good if he was dead and that looked like it was becoming more of a possibility.

Sad thing was that he couldn't even lie about this because his contact had called this morning wanting to know his next plan of action. Stupidly, Wicks had told him the truth.

Feeling a vibration in his back pocket from his cell phone, Todd jumped in surprise. It startled him so bad because he was expecting this call and dreading it more than anything in his life. He simultaneously took the cell phone out and a bandana from the other hip pocket. Wiping his forehead with the bandana, he didn't bother to look at the caller ID before answering.

"Well, is it done?"

"No." How much he hated that word at that moment.

"Well our association is at an end, Mr. Wicks. I hope you have a good life." There was a pause on the other end and then, "well what's left of it anyway," the caller chuckled.

The phone connection went silent and Wicks knew then that he had to leave and leave fast if he wanted to make it out of this alive. Slipping his cell phone in his pocket he threw what was left of his cigarette down on the ground and smashed it into the dirt. *Can't have a fire start now*, he thought ironically. Geez, he was so screwed.

Since he lived on the Baxter Ranch it would make it difficult to get his belongings, but he figured he would wait for nightfall. Parking his truck a safe distance, he could gather everything and head to Mexico after he pulled what money was left in his bank account from the advance from this job. Determining he had a plan that would hopefully work, he waited for nightfall, only a few hours away.

Making it back to his truck, Todd scanned the area just as Devon had done earlier; the only difference was that he knew that he was the only one here.

Or so he thought.

Back at the Bar B Ranch, Devon was pacing his office angrily. The sheriff had just left; the prick wouldn't know how to get out of a cardboard box without help. I mean, really, why would a man be a sheriff in Oklahoma and not know the difference in different breeds of cattle?

Devon raised some of the best Longhorns in the state; this type of breed could be used from all stages for rodeo, calves for calf roping and the yearling's for team roping and the slightly older ones used for the steer dogging. When the heifers got too old for the sport of rodeo then they were turned out to pasture and used as breeding stock. Steers followed the normal course of nature, after a certain age they were shipped to the packing plants and, if any were lucky enough to be kept as bulls, then Devon used them at the ranch or sold them to other ranchers all across the country looking for a breeding bull for their own rodeo stock.

He had turned a nice profit after college on his rodeo stock program, not to mention Longhorns didn't require as much feed being a leaner beef than most cattle. He was a cattleman that didn't make his profit from the cut of his beef, but from how well they performed in a rodeo arena.

Arrrggg. The piss ant. The city slicker fool. Not to mention not knowing anything about cattle, but to insinuate that maybe they had been mistaken about the shot taken at them. If it were the last thing Devon did, he would make sure at the next election brought about a new sheriff. Well a guy could hope anyway.

Roxie walked in to see Devon glaring out the window. "Well that went well." She smiled when she heard Devon snort. "I don't understand all this, Dev."

He turned from the window and was about to tell her some of his ideas on what was going on when they heard a knock on the door.

"Come in."

One of Devon's regular ranch hands came in shuffling his feet with his hat in his hands, not sure where to look.

"What is it, Roy?" As impatient as he was to be alone with Roxie to hash out everything that had happened today, Devon knew that he had to deal with this first. It was odd that one of his hands had come into his house.

"Um Mr. Baxter, I just wanted to let you know that I took care of Blue for you when he came into the barnyard earlier."

Devon knew the man had more to say than that; he took it for granted that his horse had made it back when he had seen Blue out in the paddock upon his and Roxie's return on Belles. "What else was there you wanted to tell me?"

Roy reached a hand up to his face and scratched his jaw and let out a deep breath and then handed Devon the piece of thin sharp metal.

"What's this?" Even though he asked the question, Devon already suspected it was the reason Blue bucked him off earlier today.

"When I unsaddled Blue earlier, he was pretty lathered so I didn't notice it until I had completely rubbed him down and I found the puncture wound on his back. So I looked at his saddle pad and noticed that this was embedded into it. It looked like it had been in the pad deeper than when I found it, that's probably why you didn't get bucked off right from the start; it took a while for it to work its way into the horse's back."

Since that was the most Devon had ever heard this man speak, he listened intently and knew that was why Blue had acted the way that he had. It made him angry that anybody would hurt a horse to get at him.

"Thank you, Roy."

As Roy started to turn and leave he was stopped by Devon's next question.

"By the way have you seen Todd today? I need to speak with him."

"Not since early this morning."

"Okay if you see him tell I need to speak with him immediately." Devon thought it odd that his foreman hadn't been seen in a while, but shrugged it off. The man could have gone into town for something.

"Will do, Mr. Baxter."

Devon turned from the door and faced Roxie and asked, "Did you call your parents and let them know what's going on?"

"Yes, the sheriff said he wanted to talk to Dad because the cattle went missing on his place, so I called him as soon as Sheriff Carter walked out the door. Dad said he'd call you as soon as the Sheriff left." Roxie watched Devon as he nodded his head in agreement, she could tell he was in deep thought and she was worried that Devon might think her dad had some part in his missing cattle. She didn't want to cause an argument, but she needed to know that he trusted her and her family.

"Devon?"

"Yeah?" By now Devon had sat down at his desk, but was staring off into space. Even though he answered automatically his mind was elsewhere. Why would anyone rob from him? And what reason did anyone have to shoot at them, unless it was one of the rustlers trying to warn them not to try and follow them.

"Devon, are you listening to me?" Realizing he wasn't listening to her, Roxie got up from her chair, moved in front of his desk and started waving her hand in front of his face trying to get his attention. Next thing she knew Devon snatched her hand and dragged her around his desk and pulled her into his lap.

"I am now. Sorry, my mind was wondering. What did you ask me?" Devon didn't really care what she wanted to know, he just didn't want her to move from his lap. So he started by moving her hair from around her neck and placing little kisses up her neck to her jaw line and nipped at her ear.

"Devon we need to have a serious talk." She wanted to say to hell with the talk, she was enjoying herself too much, but she needed to make sure he didn't blame her dad for his cattle being stolen. "Devon stop." She pushed away from him, but didn't move from his lap and he didn't take his arms from around her waist. "We need to talk about what happened today. I don't understand why someone shot at us and your cattle were stolen and all you want to do is make out."

"I'm sorry. I have a lot on my mind and I wanted a diversion." As soon as he said it, he wished he could put the words back in his mouth, especially when he saw the spark light in her eyes. Oh, she was angry.

"I'm a diversion? So would any woman do or was it just because I just happened to be handy?" Roxie slid from his lap and started pacing his office with long angry strides. She really shouldn't be this angry, it was irrational, but he wasn't talking to her about today and she needed answers.

"No Roxie. I just meant after everything that's happened today I wanted to relax with you in my arms for a while." He saw her start to relax enough that she finally stopped pacing furiously across his carpet and sat down again, only in a chair in front of his desk, so he tried to lighten the mood. "For your second question, I don't know if just any woman would have done, nobody else was here and you were handy."

Roxie knew he was teasing and tried hard to hold on to her anger, but her mouth betrayed her amusement and she put her hand up to cover the smile that was trying to form. "Idiot." She said it so low Devon wasn't sure he heard her clearly or not, but he could tell she wasn't angry anymore.

"Look I'm sorry what were you trying to ask me earlier?" They did need to talk about today. He would need to make sure that she didn't go out riding alone on the ranches until they found who was trying to shoot at them. Then he noticed that Roxie's hands had started to shake and finally he knew whatever she wanted to ask him was making her nervous, which he didn't understand.

Roxie took a deep breath and asked, "Do you suspect my dad had any reason to steal your cattle?" She hated to look at him while she asked this so she kept her eyes on the floor. What she didn't expect would be Devon's laughter. She jerked her head up to look at him and saw he was clearly amused. "And just what the heck are you laughing about?" Angry all over again that he would make light of a question that killed her to ask of him, she glared at him long and hard.

Chuckling, Devon stated so matter of fact that she didn't doubt his sincerity, "I'm laughing at the ludicrous idea that your dad would have anything to do with rustling my cattle. Please, your dad doesn't have any reason to steal. He has plenty of his own stock and money in the bank." It took him a minute to notice that Roxie was still looking at the floor like she was hoping it would swallow her up. "What aren't you telling me, Roxie?"

"All right." She knew that this was going to be hard and she had only herself to blame... maybe if she had come home sooner. "I was visiting with Mom this morning, catching up, and I asked her how the ranch was doing and she clammed up. I finally got out of her that since the price of cattle are down and everything else has gone up, Dad's been having a hard time keeping the books in the black. Dad doesn't even realize Mom knows how much of a hard time he's been having keeping the ranch afloat."

Devon leaned forward on his desk, not believing his ears. He couldn't understand why Lou hadn't come to him. The man had been like a second father to him and he hadn't known he was having financial difficulty.

Roxie watched as he took the news of her parents' ranch and asked her earlier question again, "Do you think my dad had anything to do with stealing your cattle?"

"Absolutely not. Someone just used his place as the pick up ground is all. Listen to me Roxie, I'm not going to, nor will I ever suspect your dad." He watched as relief washed over her face from the comfort of his words and hoped like hell he would never regret them.

"Thank you Devon." Roxie rose from her chair and felt she could finally breathe easy. She walked around the desk and took the back of Devon's chair pulling it away from the desk. With her hand gliding along the back and then down the side, she came to stand in front of Devon before climbing back in his lap. She watched with satisfaction as Devon's face changed from being cautious to looking every bit as if she was the tastiest morsel to come his way in a long time. Lowering her voice and whispering in his ear, she asked, "So where were we Cowboy?"

He held back a groan at her words and surprised both of them by stating, "About to take you home; it's been almost an hour and I still need to talk to your dad." As much as he wanted to stay and pick up where they had left off, he needed to make sure she got home safely before nightfall.

Amusement flickered in his eyes as he watched the surprise, then frustration come over her face. Good, now she would know how it felt.

Roxie jumped up from his lap, spun around on her heel and jabbed a finger into his chest and said, "You are the most infuriating man I know, Devon Baxter!"

He simply said, "I know." And then got up from his desk, walked to the door of his office and turned to see her staring after him. He asked, "Are you coming? It will be dark soon and we need to get you home." Chuckling, he watched as she stormed out ahead of him.

Twenty minutes later Devon cut the engine on his pickup and turned in his seat to look at Roxie. She hadn't said a word to him since they had left the house.

"Look I didn't want to bring you home anymore than you wanted to leave my house. I just want to keep you safe. Don't be mad, Honey."

Roxie took a breath and said, "I'm not mad. It's just frustrating. I feel like were teenagers again. I've been back exactly two days and all I want to do is spend my time with you and my parents are either walking in on us or you're having to take me home."

"I know how you feel Roxie; you don't know how much you've helped me in the last two days. I really could have become severely depressed after mom being killed; I felt myself sliding that way. The last two days have been frustrating for you, but they've been great for me."

Roxie instantly felt ashamed. After everything that had happened recently it was still hard to believe Lilly Baxter was gone. "I'm sorry Devon."

"Don't be." He paused then added, "I hope you won't go riding out alone until we find who's behind all this. If you feel the need then at least take a rifle with you." When she didn't say anything, he pushed. "Promise me Roxie."

"All right, I promise." She had plans to go riding tonight, but surely nothing would happen on a short ride. She would have to use another horse in the barn, since it was dark by the time they had left and both of them were coming to her parents' house, they agreed to leave Belles at his place tonight.

Later that night Roxie snuck out of the house. She chuckled to herself at her behavior. Sneaking out of her parents' house at twenty-nine years of age! It was ridiculous. Her friends in New York would laugh at the thought of it, but she had to sneak over to see Devon again.

Earlier that evening Lou and Devon had talked for hours, but had come up with no solid leads on the cattle or who was behind the shootings. She had walked him out to his truck when he was ready to go home and he had given her a good night kiss she wasn't soon to forget. Then he had asked her if she wanted to go out on a date tomorrow evening, which she happily agreed to. It would after all be their first official date and she was looking forward to it, even though she was sneaking over to his place to see him now.

He would be furious with her if he knew, but if she had anything to do about it he would get over it quick.

Saddling up an older gelding her dad had in the barn, Roxie started off across the ranch to the boundary gate between the properties. There had been a nice change in weather and it was warmer than usual, but tonight a cold front had moved in and she was shivering by the time she made it to Devon's place.

Seeing the lights still on at his house, which was surprising since it was close to eleven o'clock at night, Roxie was glad that she wouldn't have to wake him. She rode to the barn entrance and dismounted; she was just walking in when her horse gave a nervous whinny and sidestepped. "Shhh boy. I want to surprise him so don't make any noise. I'll have you unsaddled in no time."

It took a little more coaxing to get the gelding in the barn and she chalked it up to being a different place making the horse nervous, but as she walked deeper into the barn she started getting nervous herself. It was as if she wasn't alone. When she had walked about twenty feet inside, she felt something drop onto her shoulder. She was going to unsaddle the gelding without turning on the barn lights, but was too nervous to do that now. She didn't care if Devon saw the lights or not, she wanted to know what was in the barn and what had dropped on her. Roxie took the horse and put him in the side stall closest to the door. Roxie held her breath. She could feel her heart pounding. Nothing was making a sound except for the nervous shuffling from the horses' stalls. They seemed to sense something was in the air.

With her hands numb from the cold and her own fear, she found the light switch and flipped it on and then slowly turned to look inside the barn. What she saw would haunt her for the rest of her life.

Hanging from the beam in the ceiling of the barn was the body of man. The man was hanging upside down with his throat cut causing the blood to drop to the floor of the barn.

It seemed that Todd Wicks hadn't made it to Mexico after all.

Roxie started screaming.

Chapter 10

Devon was in the kitchen taking a glass out of the cabinet and filling it with water when he looked out the window. Immediately he noticed the light from the barn come on and the sound of a woman screaming sent him running to the barn.

Not having bothered to put shoes on, Devon raced barefoot across the yard to the barn enclosure. He knew his feet would be hurting tomorrow from the small rocks, but didn't give it a second thought at that moment. All he wanted was to get to the women screaming and he knew deep down that the only woman that would be on his place this late at night was Roxie.

He was angry that she would come here alone at night. Then all thoughts of his anger disappeared as he sprinted into the barn and stopped in his tracks at the sight that awaited him hanging from the ceiling.

Turning to the front inside wall of the barn he saw Roxie huddled on the floor. By now her screams had become whimpers and he could tell she couldn't seem to pull her eyes away from the gruesome sight. He dropped to the floor in front of her, but he soon realized that she didn't even know he was there.

"Roxie, Roxie listen to me! We need to get out of here and back to the house. I'm going to carry you."

Devon grunted a little. When he finally had her lifted in his arms, she was a little more than dead weight not helping him in the least. He knew she was in shock, but he didn't want to waste the time here to get her to snap out of it. He had never been a man that was bothered by the sight of blood, but the contents in his stomach were threatening to come back up if had to look at the sight of the bloody body in his barn again.

Having raced out only in his boxers and a t-shirt he was shivering from the cool night air by the time he got them both back in the house. Setting Roxie down in one of the kitchen chairs, he went to shut and lock all the doors and windows before doing anything else. On his way back to the kitchen, he grabbed the cordless phone. In no time, he was sitting down in a chair alongside Roxie, who was shivering violently by now.

Making the first call to the police department, he filled the dispatcher in on the emergency and requested extra units out to the ranch as fast as possible to scan the area. It felt like someone was still out there watching, waiting. Waiting for what? He didn't know, but he would find out and he needed to find out quick.

That cursed woman, she had almost seen him. She had rode up to the barn as he barely got around the outside corner of the barn. He shouldn't have been here and he wouldn't have needed to be if that fool Wicks had done his job. Since Wicks hadn't completed the job, he had to take care of him personally.

After she entered the barn, he took off through the woods at the back of the barn. He only paused long enough to hear the scream rip through the silence of the night and he didn't bother looking over his shoulder toward the sound. He just continued on his way back to where his truck was left parked a few miles away, only now he had a knowing smile on his face. He slowed his pace as he came closer to his truck. All around him he heard the sounds of the woods. The slight breeze through the still bare limbs of the trees overhead, to the nocturnal animals that were nosing around looking for their nightly meal, these things bothered most people. He wasn't like most people.

Looking back once more in the direction of where the ranch house was located, the man knew in his soul that it would be only a matter of time before all of it belonged to him, like it should have years ago. He knew there were only two people that would need to be taken care in order to get what he wanted and what he wanted was this ranch. No, that wasn't quite right; he wanted the ranch, but it was really just a means to an end. This was personal and he'd waited almost thirty years for this day and nothing would stop him from taking everything away from Devon Baxter. If the Lancaster woman got in the way, he wouldn't mind putting her in a grave with him.

Enough of that; now because of that insipid foreman he'd killed, he not only had to re-evaluate his plans, he needed to do something with the several head of cattle that Wicks had stolen. He didn't need any attention drawn to him so he couldn't sell them. Not that he needed the money anyway, he didn't. So he figured he would hire a couple of men to load them up and release them a few miles from the ranch or just keep them hidden for awhile. If nothing else came of it, confusion and speculation would arise as to what was going on. Which didn't bother him because he knew that nobody could place the blame on him for either the stolen cattle or the murder. How do you blame someone that doesn't exist?

Finally reaching his pickup, the man got in and started the ignition. He turned the heater up to ward off the chill in the night air not having noticed it until then because he'd been riding on the adrenaline of killing Wicks and getting away from the barn without being seen. Now to get back to his place for some sleep and a shower; tomorrow would be a new day with all new possibilities.

Back at the Bar B Ranch, Devon was trying to get Roxie to stop shaking. After calling the police, he decided to take her to the living

Eternal Peace

room and lay her on the couch. When she seemed somewhat OK, he went to fetch a snifter of whiskey.

Crouching down on the floor in front of the couch, he lifted her head up enough and said, "Roxie, Honey you need to drink some of this; it will help calm your nerves."

Roxie took a sip of the drink and nearly gagged. It had been a long time since she'd had a drink of whiskey and it wasn't a pleasant experience, but it brought her back to her senses and she looked a Devon and whispered, "I can't believe it."

"I know, me neither." Devon didn't raise his voice above a whisper hoping to soothe her. She didn't say anything else. Devon's mind, however, was spinning. He didn't understand what was going on. He especially couldn't figure out why his foreman was murdered in his barn. Was Wicks involved in his cattle being stolen? Was he the one shooting at them today? He hoped that the police could shed some light on some of these questions. The ringing of the telephone interrupted his thoughts and made them both jump.

Having brought the cordless phone with him earlier from the kitchen, he answered it on the second ring expecting to hear from the police. Surprisingly though it was his father. "Dad, is something wrong?"

"No, can't your father call home to check on things?"

"Of course, I'm sorry Dad. I'm just a little stressed."

Noticing the strain in his son's voice, John asked, "What's wrong?"

"Todd Wicks was murdered tonight. We're waiting on the police to get here."

After several seconds of silence, Devon asked, "Dad?"

"Yeah son, I'm here. What happened and what's this we business, who else is there with you?"

"I honestly don't know why Wicks was killed, it's been a rough couple of days. Hell, it's been a rough couple of weeks, Dad. Roxie is the person with me; she came home." As he said her name he felt her stiffen, but relax as he put his hand on her hair and started stroking it to relax her. He was sitting on the couch with Roxie's head resting on his lap. He closed his eyes and leaned his head back against the couch and explained to his father everything that had happened in the last few days. As he ended, Devon heard the sirens of police cars in the distance and relief washed over him. "Dad the cops are almost here. I need to go. Where are you?"

"Don't worry about it. I'll be home as soon as I can and everything will be back to normal," John stated gruffly.

Devon looked at the phone when he heard the dial tone, thinking his father sounded a bit unusual but shrugged it off to grief. Setting down the phone on the side table next to the couch Devon got up to answer the door. "The police are here, Roxie. Are you going to be all right for a few minutes while I go let them in?"

The knocking on the door was getting persistent now and so Roxie answered in a low voice, "Go, I want this over with as soon as possible."

"Me too, Honey," Devon stated and turned to sprint to the front door.

The next few hours was grueling for both of them. By the time the police and the medical examiner had left, Roxie and Devon were both exhausted. During the interrogation by the officers, Devon and Roxie had to be placed in different rooms of Devon's house to give separate statements. Roxie was grateful that her parents had showed up not long after Devon called them so she at least had someone to sit with her during the last few hours to help her cope with recalling her story.

By now it was almost two thirty in the morning and even though they were all exhausted they were also too keyed up to simply sleep. Milly had taken over Devon's kitchen and made everyone coffee and some sandwiches and they all sat in Devon's living room rehashing what the medical examiner and Sheriff Carter had informed them about Wicks' death.

"I know I've said it before, but I simply can't believe this has happened," Roxie said at last, her voice filling the seemingly endless silence.

"I know. If what the medical examiner thinks is true then when you rode up to the barn it was only minutes after Wicks had been killed." Devon was still shaken by the fact that Roxie had come so close and thankfully had not become a target herself. "You're sure that you didn't see anything at all?" Devon hated asking because he knew that the cops had already grilled her enough tonight.

Upon Devon asking the question, Roxie dropped her head forward on her knees and simply let out an exhausted breath. "I'm sure Devon. I didn't know anything was wrong until I got in the barn." After saying this she couldn't help the involuntary shudder that racked through her body at the memory of what she had seen tonight.

"Okay Roxie, I know we're all exhausted. I think we all need to get some sleep. Lou, Milly you're both welcome to stay here tonight. I know this probably isn't the ideal place right know to spend the night, but it might be a good idea to stick together until we find out what is going on."

Lou surprised everybody with his answer. "Actually I think we will stay."

"You're sure?" Devon asked.

Lou looked over at where Devon was sitting with Roxie on the loveseat and stated simply, "I think it's best if we all stay in one place and since Roxie left to come see you tonight maybe we can all sleep better knowing that everybody is safely under one roof, but just for tonight. Frankly I'm just too tired to go back home even though we don't live very far away." Lou knew it was the right decision by the relief on Milly and Roxie's faces and appreciation on Devon's. Even though Devon had grown into an impressive young man, he didn't deserve to have everyone desert him tonight, especially with a murderer on the loose.

Devon realized in that moment that even though he had just lost his mother and his father had left he wasn't without family; he had his second family here with him and, if Roxie agreed, he could make it legal and not feel so alone all the time. Although Roxie would probably claim his decision was based on sheer exhaustion, he cleared his throat and watched as Roxie picked her head up from her knees and looked at him with a question in her eyes. She knew him well enough to know that he always cleared his throat before he was about to admit something that he was nervous about. She smiled at the memories that flooded back.

With Roxie looking at him, Devon got up from his seat and said, "If you'll excuse me a minute; I know were all tired, but if you'll bare with me just one more second." With that Devon left the room.

"What was that all about, Roxie?" Milly asked. Both of Roxie's parents looked at her questioningly.

" I have no idea, but the only time he clears his throat is when he has something to say that he's nervous about. Right now I'm just too tired to speculate." At that moment Devon walked back in the room with a sheepish look on his face.

Striding up to Roxie and sitting back down next to her on the sofa, he unclenched what was in his hand and heard a gasp from Milly as he held out the black velvet box to Roxie.

Clearing his throat again he looked into Roxie's eyes and noticed she was blushing. He smiled at her and asked the one question he had waited most of his life to ask. Trying to ignore the surprised looks on her parents' faces, he took Roxie's hand and placed the box in her hand. He said huskily, "Believe me I know with what has happened the last few days and especially tonight this could possibly be the worst moment in history to do this, but I simply can't help it. Roxie, you've made your feelings explicitly clear to me since you've come home and I know you wanted me to take time before I told you in turn how I felt about you, but what you don't know is this ring has been waiting eleven years for you, just as I've been waiting eleven years to give it to you."

"Oh Devon..." Roxie began, but Devon cut her short.

"No... let me finish, please. This is hard enough. You know I'm not good with expressing what I feel; I've been told too many times that I've become a hard man to know. I became even worse after I realized you weren't coming home, but you're back and I don't want you to leave. I can't be alone Roxie and I've felt that way since you left. You are my best friend, but more importantly, you are my soul mate." He paused to take a breath before saying the next words that he promised he would tell her if he ever saw her again.

"I love you Roxie. Will you marry me?" He knew she loved him, but he also knew she had a life in New York that was as much a part of her as her past was here.

Roxie didn't know if she started crying from being completely exhausted or the fact that she had waited for those words from Devon for so long; she only knew that this had been the worst night of her life until now and there was no way she was letting him slip through her fingers. Smiling through her tears she could only nod her head and take the beautiful diamond ring from the box and slip it on her finger.

Chapter 11

So engrossed in what had just happened, Roxie forgot about her parents being in the room. Still crying and leaning forward to give Devon a kiss, she jumped when surprisingly her mother jumped up from her seat and started yelling, "Woohoo! Finally!"

Grinning from ear to ear her father joined her mother and they started dancing around the room joyously.

Devon and Roxie just gaped at them and then started laughing when they realized that, once again, a special moment between the two of them had been interrupted.

Then, as if a switch had been turned off, all the laughter died in the room as everyone seemed to simultaneously remember the events that had led up to this moment and that there was a body laying in the morgue with the killer still on the loose.

"Despite this wonderful news, I think given the circumstances and the fact that it's so late maybe we should all get some sleep and discuss everything in the morning," Lou stated.

At this everybody nodded solemnly and then Milly asked, "Devon if you would tell us which guest room to use? We'll leave you two alone." By this time Roxie's parents had been edging towards the door of the living room ready to make their exit.

"Of course. If you'll just go to the top of the stairs and pick the last door on the left you both should have everything you need.

Eternal Peace

Mom even kept extra sleepwear for guests in case they found themselves forgetting something. Just look in the drawers of the dresser. The adjoining bathroom is stocked also."

Both nodded as they left the room to let Devon know that they had heard him.

Finally alone at last Devon turned back around to Roxie and said, "So I thought…" He let out a breath along with the rest of what he was going to say because Roxie was fast asleep, her head leaning against the side of the couch she was sitting on.

"Geez, what does a guy have to do to catch a break?" Devon looked up at the ceiling and then back down at Roxie. He let out another breath. Chuckling, he moved over to the couch and bent down to scoop Roxie up into his arms.

Even though Lou and Milly were staying in his house tonight, he wasn't leaving Roxie in a guestroom by herself. He would at least get to sleep with his fiancé, literally. He'd take what he could get at this point. Smiling, he made his way to his bedroom and placed Roxie on the bed long enough to pull one side of the covers back. Then, shifting her to that side and covering her up, he watched as she wriggled in her sleep to get a better position and he knew this night would be torture for him.

Down the hall Roxie's parents were settling in for sleep when Milly turned worriedly to her husband and asked, "Should we have left them alone? I mean do you think that Devon will put her in another room besides his?" She knew she sounded overprotective, but she was Roxie's mother after all.

A deep chuckle met her question and Lou answered, "If you want to be the one to go and ask Devon where he's putting our daughter for the night be my guest." Feeling Milly tense beside him, he hurriedly explained his amusement. He just wanted to get some sleep at this point. "Look, Honey, as much as I hate that he might place Roxie in his room because of obvious reasons that I don't want to discuss I think were all tired and exhausted tonight and she'll be safer with Devon. If it makes you feel any better just get up early in the morning and announce breakfast outside their door."

"That's a good idea." Finally relaxed they both drifted off to sleep.

Roxie woke to an arm draped across her waist and couldn't understand who was with her until she realized she was in Devon's bedroom. She had slept what little of the night that was left in Devon's bed and she didn't even know how she had got there and frankly didn't care. Rolling over, which wasn't easy because Devon's arm kept tightening around her to keep her in place, she finally rolled over enough to see his face relaxed in sleep and couldn't believe they were finally alone; she was going to relish this.

Lifting her hand to his face she skimmed her fingertips along his profile still not believing she was finally here. She then noticed the ring on her finger and a swell of happiness bubbled up inside her because she knew that it hadn't been a dream that he had truly proposed to her. Within seconds her happiness shifted into fear as she also remembered the other events of last night. She tried to keep a shudder from going through her body at the memory. Instead, focusing on the good things that had happened, she looked back at Devon's face and was startled that he was looking at her sleepily.

"Good mornin', Cowboy," Roxie said, sleep lacing her voice making it sound huskier than normal.

"Good mornin', Honey. I hope that frown on your face a second ago wasn't a second thought to my proposal?" Although he was exhausted from only a few hours of sleep, he was still hoping that she wouldn't regret agreeing to marry him after only being home for a few days.

Letting a smile come over her face she shook her head and told him why she had been frowning and that she was ecstatic about their engagement.

Smiling at each other, Devon leaned closer and took Roxie's mouth with his and tightened his hold on her waist to bring her as close as possible. Moving her beneath him, he realized he had definitely been a gentlemen by putting her to bed completely clothed and needed her naked as soon as possible.

Breathlessly, Roxie tore her mouth away from Devon's and said, "I have way too many clothes on. What are you going to do about it?"

With a devilish gleam entering his green eyes and without answering her with words, Devon started removing her clothes as fast as possible.

When all he had left to take off was her panties, what there actually was of them being only a small scrap of pale pink silk, he paused and looked his fill of her luscious body and ached all over from wanting her so bad.

"You don't realize how much I want you. I have always wanted you," Devon whispered huskily in Roxie's ear making her shiver with anticipation.

Taking his hand and placing it on her hip he started to slowly lower her underwear down to reveal his most treasured goal.

With both of them so wrapped up in each other it took a few seconds to realize that someone was knocking on the bedroom door.

"Are you two awake?" Milly asked and without waiting for an answer she said, "Breakfast will be ready shortly so don't take your time. Get down to the kitchen so it doesn't get cold," Milly said feeling sure that they were awake and had heard her. She smiled and proceeded to the kitchen to start breakfast.

In the bedroom Devon started cursing a blue streak and pounding his fist against the pillow beside Roxie's head.

Roxie was struggling not to laugh. Here was a grown man having a temper tantrum because his soon to be mother-in-law had interrupted them, again.

"Shhh, it will be okay. I swear we'll have our time alone... hopefully." Roxie started giggling and couldn't stop. Oh how the last few days had been so crazy.

"I hope you aren't laughing, because if you are I'm afraid you'll have to face the consequences," Devon said, all this while his face was buried in the pillow, muffling his voice. Hearing Milly's voice on the other side of the bedroom door had been a surprise to him because, frankly, he had forgotten all about anything but Roxie.

Propping himself up on his elbow to look down into Roxie's eyes, Devon stated blandly, "Hell, I hate to say it Roxie, but I might just have to ban your parents from ever stepping foot in my house again." Devon's mouth broke into a smirk and then he burst out laughing at the ridiculous situation. At that Roxie let go with a belly laugh and shoved Devon off her.

"Come on, we had better get dressed and go to the kitchen before mom sends my dad up here to round us up." Roxie had slid off the bed and was picking up her clothes where Devon had thrown them. She had given up on any modesty she might have had; it was no use anyway. Devon hadn't moved from his position on the bed, he was steadily watching her get dressed.

He really was a handsome man. He had a hard toned body from all the ranch work that he did, gorgeous black hair and those emerald green eyes that were currently looking at her as if she was the only thing he wanted at that moment, but knew he couldn't have and that made it all the sweeter.

"I guess I'll just have to settle for watching you get dressed, a striptease in reverse."

Roxie blushed wishing she could just take her clothes back off and climb back into bed for the rest of the day.

"Come on, lazy. Let's go downstairs." Slapping him on the rear on the way to the door, "You know you really do have a nice butt, Dev."

At that Devon rolled over unashamedly and claimed, "Other parts of me are even nicer, but I guess you'll have to find out some other time." He watched as Roxie turned an even brighter red. She fumbled with the doorknob and tried without much success to leave with dignity, but it didn't last.

"I'll be down in a minute, you go ahead Roxie."

"Okay." But just as she was leaving she turned back and crossed the room and reached up to nibble on Devon's lower lip, then kissed him quickly and left the room.

"Darn it, she's going to be the death of me," he said to the now empty bedroom.

Ten minutes later Devon entered the kitchen to find everybody just sitting down to breakfast. It brought back memories of his own mother being in this very kitchen fixing him and his father their morning meals before going out to the ranch duties.

"Devon? Are you all right?" Lou asked noticing how Devon's jaw had tightened as he had entered the kitchen.

"Yeah, sorry. I was just thinking of mom," Devon said somberly.

After that no one said anything. They just started eating the food Milly had laid out for everyone. When they had all finished up, they all helped to clear the dishes and before long the kitchen was straightened up and all four of them sat back down and decided to spend time discussing what had happened last night since they were all alert this morning from much needed sleep.

Filling coffee cups and bringing them to the table, Roxie sat down next to Devon and asked, "Do you have any idea about what's going on here? Who would steal your cattle, shoot at us and kill your foreman?"

"I have no idea." Just then, Devon heard a car door slam and, seconds later, footsteps on the porch. Devon got up from his seat just as the person started knocking on the door.

On the porch stood Sheriff Carter, his hat in his hand. He was looking serious. "Can we talk a minute? I thought I would fill you in on some details, at least on what we have so far, which isn't much at this point."

"Of course. Come in for some coffee. Roxie and her parents are here also. You can fill us all in."

Nodding his head, the sheriff entered the house and followed Devon through to the kitchen where everyone else was sitting having coffee. "Good morning everyone."

The sheriff took a seat and thanked Roxie for the cup of coffee. He took a breath. "Look, first I wanted to apologize for the other day when I suggested that Mr. Baxter and Ms. Lancaster here may not have been shot at; it was unprofessional."

"It still pisses me off that you didn't believe us before and it's taken somebody to be murdered for you to take notice," Devon said heatedly, not bothering with politeness.

Ducking his head the sheriff truly looked embarrassed and Roxie felt sorry for him. She placed a hand on Devon's forearm and said, "We need all the help we can get now Devon, please let it go. He's making an effort now."

Letting out a sigh Devon turned back to the sheriff and said, "Fine. We accept your apology. Now what have you figured out on Wicks' murder and my cattle?"

"Not much. We do know that Wicks is the one that shot at you."

Devon was so surprised he almost dropped his coffee mug in his lap. "Are you sure?"

"Yeah, we found a shell casing by a tree in the general direction you gave us and it was a match to Wicks' rifle. It's only logical that he helped in stealing your cattle and was trying to warn the two of you away."

"So where are my cattle?" Devon was trying to process this information. He had known Wicks for several years and still couldn't believe that his foreman had anything to do with the missing cattle, but apparently the evidence was leading them that way.

"We still don't know where your cattle are, Mr. Baxter. Wicks obviously had help and they were probably the ones that killed him."

"So you don't know anything about Wicks' murderer yet?" Lou asked when no one else said anything.

"No. Whoever killed him was thorough; he didn't even leave tracks in your barn. Everything was swept clean, except for both of your tracks of course. Plus, whoever killed him is sending a message to someone and I think it's personal towards you Mr. Baxter."

Even more taken back, Devon didn't know what to say.

The sheriff went on. "Do you have any enemies that you know of Devon? Anybody at all? I would advise making a list of potential people that you've royally pissed off recently or over the years."

"I can't take this all in; I mean this is crazy." Devon was exasperated.

"Well the only other theory is that it was just a plain cattle rustling operation gone wrong and that your ranch was involved."

"So what do we do now?" Roxie asked.

"We'll keep looking for any clues that will help us find who did this, but in the meantime I ask that if you see or hear anything, even the smallest little thing, let us know immediately. We don't want anybody else hurt." Noticing how close Devon and Roxie were sitting and the way she kept trying to comfort him, he wondered if there was something between the two. As far as he knew, Roxie had left years ago. Her returning home a few days ago was suspicious in itself.

"Ms. Lancaster, may I ask why you've just now returned home?" The sheriff watched surprise come over her face watching to see if she might be guilty of anything he could pick up on.

"It's a long story... and personal."

"Why don't you explain it to me anyway?" He felt bad starting to drill her about her past, but he needed to know everything about anyone that had come into Peace lately, especially someone that had stayed away all this time. The sheriff couldn't help but notice the gleam in her eye. *She is one beautiful woman,* he thought to himself. *She's not that much younger than I am. Maybe I could take her out sometime... that is if she wasn't attached to Devon. It would be just my luck.*

"Why is her story relevant to you, sheriff? The point is that she's back now and for good." Devon didn't like how the sheriff had started looking at her, so he added, "We are engaged and she'll be moving in here when we get married."

Sheriff Carter tensed and, not liking the smug tone that had come into Devon Baxter's voice, said, "I see. Well I think I would still like to hear the story. She can tell me here or I can take her in and she can tell me in town." He was starting to get pissed and realized he needed to back off before he stepped out of line. Even though he was the sheriff, he knew that the Baxters had a lot of influence in Peace and the surrounding areas, but shoot, he hated arrogant rich ranchers and he knew that Baxter resented him already because he wasn't raised in the country.

"I think you can leave now sheriff. If we hear or see anything else we'll let you know," Devon said coldly, not taking his eyes off the man until he saw him squirm in his seat. Even though the sheriff was older than him, Devon knew he could take him if need be.

"Fine, but if I feel it's relevant later to further investigation I will request her story and be damned to you, Baxter." Sheriff Carter got up and started towards the back door.

"We'll see, sheriff," Devon said sarcastically.

Not having said much since the sheriff had arrived, Lou piped up. "Son, I think you're not only going to have trouble from Wicks' killer, but from that idiot sheriff too."

"I think you maybe right, Lou"

"Why was the sheriff acting that way? It was unnerving," Roxie stated. She was glad that he had finally left. He had only brought more tension.

"Well it's one of two things: he was either truly interested in your whereabouts for the last eleven years and why you had showed up back home or he's interested in you personally," Devon stated angrily.

"That's crazy. He doesn't even know me." Roxie didn't believe it. Devon and her father were crazy for thinking of such an idiotic idea. The man was just trying to do his job and investigate a murder, but she really didn't relish telling her story to a stranger.

With everyone still at the kitchen table reflecting on the sheriff's visit, Milly looked at her husband and finally spoke up. "Lou, I think it's time we go home."

"Yeah I agree. Roxie are you ready to go? I'm sure you could use a change of clothes."

Roxie let out a breath. She knew the next thing she said wouldn't be welcome at the moment, but she knew she needed to say it. There were things that needed to be taken care of and if the sheriff was sniffing around her about her story he really wouldn't like knowing what she was going to do next, but there was no help for it.

Noticing that Roxie hadn't answered her father, Devon thought maybe she wanted to tell them she was going to stay here even though they hadn't talked about that yet. He was about to open his mouth when Roxie turned to look at him and knocked him flat with her next statement.

"No, I mean yes I need to go home and get a change of clothes, but I also need to pack," Roxie stated in a rush watching as anger filled Devon's face. "I'm going back to New York."

Chapter 12

Shoving back his chair, which toppled to the floor with a loud thump Devon yelled, "The hell you are!"

Roxie realized then that maybe she should have explained a little bit more about her trip before blurting in out that way. She started to smile over the misunderstanding, but glanced across the table at her parents and up at Devon and knew she better explain and fast.

"Okay, I might have said that a bit hastily."

"You think?" Devon said sarcastically.

"I need to go back to New York, but not to stay," Roxie said watching her mom and dad let out their breath. She knew she had truly hurt them more than she thought if they were so worried that if she mentioned going somewhere they thought she wouldn't be coming back. She could see that Devon was extremely tense standing beside her. "Look, since Devon and I are getting married, I thought I would go back and settle my life there so that I could move back permanently. Devon, I didn't mean to imply that I was leaving for good."

Devon walked away from the table and leaned against the kitchen counter. He let out a breath he hadn't realize he'd been holding. He had overreacted. "I'm sorry I yelled at you, it's just hard for me to let you leave."

Eternal Peace

Roxie looked at everyone at the table individually so that they would know that when she spoke it was with sincerity. "I will come back, I promise."

Lou looked at his daughter that he loved so much. He didn't want her to leave again, but he knew that she needed to let go of her past to make her future with Devon. "All right, it's just hard for us. Do you want one of us to go with you?"

"No Dad, but thanks for the offer. It won't take me more than a few days to a week at the most to take care of my job, apartment and things." Roxie looked over at Devon and wondered what he was thinking. It didn't take long to find out.

"I'm going with you."

"No, Devon." Roxie was shaking her head.

"Yes, Roxie. I'm going to help you move and make sure you come back."

Roxie was starting to get completely fed up with how they were all treating her. She wasn't a child and could take care of herself, which was exactly what she had been doing for the last eleven years without any of their help. Getting up from her chair and walking to the other side of the kitchen, she faced Devon and said angrily, "I'm going by myself and all of you need to trust that I will come back. I know I left all those years ago and didn't come home and I've gave you all my heartfelt apologies about the past. Frankly Devon, if you can't trust me enough to go on a trip so that I can come back to our future then maybe I need to rethink marrying you." Taking the ring off her finger was the hardest thing she had to do, but she slipped it off and handed it to Devon.

Watching Devon's face go from anger to paleness from her statement, she hoped she hadn't pushed him too far. "Besides, aren't you forgetting what happened last night? You have more than enough on your plate at the moment and with the sheriff acting the way he is, it probably wouldn't be the best idea if you left with me."

Milly spoke just then to Devon. "Devon, I know you don't want her to go, we don't want her to go either, but she'll come back." Pausing for a second she went on to say, "Roxie, we do trust you. You're our daughter and we worry is all."

All this time Roxie's hand had still been holding out the ring, hoping that Devon trusted her enough not to take the ring from her.

Devon looked down at the ring and then back at Roxie's face, he said, "That ring doesn't belong anywhere but on that finger and everything that I said to you last night stands." Watching her slip the ring back on, he felt he could relax. Geez, he had almost screwed everything up when it was finally coming together. "Look, I trust you and I'm sorry if I made you feel that way. However hard it will be to say goodbye to you for however short a time, I'll know I can't wait till I'll get to see you again. So go take the time you need and come back to me, to all of us."

Trying not to cry over the entire situation she said, "I love you, Devon. I can't wait to start our life together."

"I know, me too."

Hearing her parents pushing back their chairs and coming around the table, she said, "I want to get an early start and leave today so I'd better go."

"Come here for a second." Holding his arms out for her to come to him, he looked past her and asked, "Will you two give us a minute? She'll be right out."

As Lou and Milly walked out the back door, Roxie walked to Devon and threw her arms around him, pressing her face against his chest. Neither one spoke, they just wrapped their arms around each other. "Roxie?"

"Yeah?" Looking up, she heard the strain in Devon's voice.

"Please come back to me. I love you." Devon hated feeling vulnerable, but he needed her to know how he felt for her. He only hoped it was enough for her to give up everything in New York.

Rising up on her toes Roxie kissed him and said, "I make this promise: nothing will keep me from coming back to you." With one more kiss Roxie turned and walked to the door, turning before opening the door she said, "Goodbye, Cowboy, I'll see you in a week."

"Goodbye, Honey. Call me with your return information and I'll pick you up from the airport." Devon gave a little wave as she nodded and left. He had a bad feeling about this trip. She thought that he didn't trust her and maybe deep down there was some truth to that, but with Wicks' murder and the missing cattle Devon felt something more was going to happen. He just didn't know how to avoid it and he was very much afraid of not being able to protect her.

Shaking his head over the fact that maybe he was being paranoid, he took out his cell phone and decided to call his father... another person that was worrying him. It rang for a while and then went to voicemail. Devon left a message asking his father to call him back when possible. He wanted to know when to expect his dad. Slipping his phone back in his back pocket, he headed outside. The ranch hands had probably already come to work and were wondering about the crime scene tape on the outside of the barn. He'd have to explain to them.

Walking across the yard to the outer buildings he noticed his men, five in total, hanging around the horse pens. As he walked toward them they all straightened, waiting for him to speak.

"Men, I don't know if you've heard what happened last night or not," Devon said. He halted when Billy Burns stepped forward and said, "Sir, we know what happened. The cops showed up last night at all our houses and woke us up asking for our statements and about Mr. Wicks."

Devon hadn't thought about the cops questioning his men, but it made sense that they would. "Okay, well do any of you have any questions?"

Burns must have been appointed spokesman this morning by all of them because he asked, "Who's the new foreman?" and then looked embarrassed for asking. "I mean we need to know who to go through when you're not around."

Devon hadn't thought about it much, but he didn't feel right about stepping any of the hands up to that position yet because of what was going on; he didn't know if any of his other men were involved in the stealing or the killing. "Right now no one will be new foreman, everything will go through me."

For a moment it looked as if Billy was going to object. Devon had known Billy for as long as he could remember. They were both the same age and Devon knew that Billy probably had some resentment for working for him. He wondered if Billy had any part of what had happened on the ranch the last few days. Devon asked next, "Do you have a problem with me being the boss of my own ranch or do you feel the need to object, Mr. Burns?"

Looking angry for being called on the spot about Devon's decision, Burns let his anger show for a second, but decided it would only end in him getting fired. He needed this job, since all he knew was Cowboy work. As much as it pissed him off that it wasn't his ranch and he would need to accept any decision Devon made for now. He had been hoping to become foreman because of the pay raise that came with it, something he desperately needed. "No Mr. Baxter, no problem; it's your place."

"Now to start, if there's anything that you need answers for you can come in the house and knock on my office doors if I'm home. If I'm gone, feel free to call my cell phone anytime for any reason... even if you think you see something suspicious don't hesitate to call me. Furthermore, I'm issuing ranch cell phones to everybody so that we can all have access to each other at any time." He looked at all the men to see if he was going to have any problems, but nobody seemed to mind.

"What about the barn, Mr. Baxter? Can we go in there?"

Devon looked at Stuart, the man that had spoken, and noticed the man glancing towards the barn as if it was the last place he wanted to go. Devon made a decision.

"If any of you men don't feel comfortable going in the barn just yet, I'll understand." As he said this, he watched as a smirk came over Burns' face and made another decision that wouldn't earn him any favors. "Come to think of it, Burns, you seem to not have a problem with going in there so Stuart's duties will be yours this week." He watched as the smirk left Billy's face. Burns swallowed, turning his head to look at the barn with the yellow crime scene tape fluttering in the breeze.

Clearly angry, Billy turned and stomped off towards the cattle barn that was separate from the horse barn and disappeared inside the building. Stuart came up to Devon looking uncomfortable and shuffling his feet.

"I don't want anybody angry at me, Mr. Baxter. I can do my own duties. It just makes me nervous to go in there, but I'll get over it."

Devon looked towards the horse barn where Wicks was murdered and an involuntary shudder worked down his spine from the memory of last night. He turned his head to look back at Stuart before answering. "Stuart, believe me you have nothing to worry about. I don't even want to go in there, but that feeling will fade with time and Mr. Burns needs a lesson in humility." He paused and then said, "If he gives you any trouble let me know, but for now you take over his duties for the week. Can you handle his schedule?"

Still looking uncomfortable, but appreciative of his decision about the barn, Stuart looked at Devon and answered positively. "Yes sir I can."

"Good. I'll be in my office catching up on some business that I've slacked on for the last few weeks."

"Umm, sir? I know it's a little late, but I wanted to offer my condolences on your mother's passing."

Looking down at the ground, Devon said, "It's all right. I appreciate the sentiment. I think you can tell everyone that congratulations are now in order, I'm getting married soon."

Surprised, but glad for the change in subject Stuart said, "Of course. Congratulations! I'm guessing it was the lady that brought you in on that pretty buckskin yesterday that's still in the barn. The neighbor's daughter, Roxie Lancaster?"

"Yes. Well, we need to get to work." Turning before the conversation got any more involved, Devon walked off back towards the house. He was trying to keep himself from actually going after Roxie. He knew it was important to her to take care of everything in New York and he also wouldn't have to keep a look out for her safety from whoever had killed Wicks, so maybe it was a blessing that she was going on the trip. He just wished his gut would agree with his head. He was still feeling as if she would be in danger even if she left.

He also hoped that he didn't have to watch his back with his own ranch hands, but he knew that he needed to. Burns especially made him uneasy, but maybe it was just the tension he'd been feeling since all of this had started.

Taking his cell phone from his pocket again he dialed his father, but still didn't get an answer. He wished his father would call him back. Even though they hadn't always been close, it would still make him feel more comfortable if he knew his dad was here. Making it to his house and office he sat down at his desk and tried to concentrate on the ranch books for the day.

Meanwhile, Roxie was currently sitting on her bed with her cell phone. She had just called the airline and booked a ticket, the only one she could get would leave at five in the morning. Her mother was currently packing her bags for her, fussing over everything. She didn't want to take them away from home long so she called a hotel she had looked up online that was closest to the airport.

Eternal Peace

After she made the reservation, she noticed her mom was looking at her questionably about making a hotel reservation.

"Since my flight leaves so early in the morning I was hoping you and dad could take me to the city and I would spend the night at the hotel so that none of us had to get up early to make the flight."

"Oh, well that makes sense. We'll take you to dinner this evening in the city after you check in."

"Sounds like a plan. Now let's get me packed, which shouldn't take long since I've been here only two days," Roxie laughed.

Later that day, with Roxie checked into her hotel, the group decided to go to a steakhouse before her parents headed back home. Entering the restaurant, Roxie noticed her dad looking over his shoulder and wondered why he had a puzzled look on his face.

"What is it Dad?" Roxie looked across the street, but didn't see anything out of the ordinary.

"I could have sworn I saw somebody we knew." Shaking his head, Lou continued into the restaurant. The hostess directed them to their seats.

After getting settled, Milly asked, "Who was it that you thought you recognized?"

Half listening to her father's answer, Roxie was pouring over the menu when her father said unexpectedly, "John Baxter, but I can't be sure with it almost being dark outside."

Roxie lifted her head from the menu and asked, "You think it was Mr. Baxter?"

"Well it looked like him, but no I can't be sure," Lou said.

Roxie was shaking her head and said, "No Dad, I bet you did see him because he called last night right after we found Wicks in the barn and Devon talked to him. I wasn't thinking all that clearly, but I do remember that his dad was coming home. It probably was him you saw."

"Well that explains it then. Do you want to call Devon and tell him that we spotted his father?" Milly asked.

"No. I don't know Mr. Baxter's plans and I don't want to give Devon false information, especially if it turns out to not be him," Roxie said. "Now let's eat; I'm so hungry. What are you guys going to have?" Roxie forced a smile to her face. She was trying to take her mind off Devon and his father. If it was Baxter Senior, Roxie wished he would be going home as soon as possible. She didn't like to think Devon was on the ranch alone even though she knew he could take care of himself.

Lou chuckled and said, "Well, we are in a steakhouse in Oklahoma so I think steaks are in order."

"Ha ha Dad, I was just trying to make conversation," Roxie said.

A few minutes later they had ordered and were waiting on their food when Roxie glanced towards the door. She was shocked to see one of her co-workers, Brandon Wiley. As the hostess was showing him to a table, he glanced in her direction and she noted the surprise on his face as he spotted her also. Some suited men accompanied him and it was obvious that he was on a business meeting, but she was still shocked to see him here.

Excusing himself from the group, Brandon made his way to their table. "Roxie?"

"Brandon, what are you doing here?"

"I'd ask the same thing, but I know you took a leave of absence. We all figured you had come home for a while, but I didn't expect to see you here. I'm here on business as you can see." As he said this he motioned towards the table where the men were waiting on him.

"Brandon, these are my parents." She made the introduction and then said, "I'm heading back to New York in the morning."

"Well your leave of absence wasn't very long, but we'll be glad to have you back at work… especially me," Brandon said.

Roxie was hoping he would avoid talking about their past relationship in front of her parents, but could tell that was hopeless now. "Yes, well I'll still be on leave. I just have business that needs taking care of and then I will be heading back here." She paused and then said, "Permanently, Brandon"

Brandon tensed and said, "What about us Roxie? You can't just leave New York and not come back. You'll miss it too much."

Exasperated that this conversation was taking place in front of her parents, Roxie said, "There is no us. We broke up over a year ago; let it go." Roxie had to admit the only thing she had seen in Brandon was his looks and that was probably because he favored Devon so much, only his hair was a shade lighter and he had blue eyes, not green.

"I see. Well I was just hoping is all. If you will all excuse me, I've left my party waiting for too long as it is." With that they watched Brandon join his table and avoid looking in their direction for the remainder of their meal.

Roxie looked at her parents' faces and said, "Sorry about that." She didn't think there was anything else to say about the situation. She watched as her parents glanced at each other and couldn't resist asking, "What is it you want to ask?"

After a few seconds and a glance over at Brandon, Milly said, "Well we can't help noticing the resemblance between that man and Devon. I mean we know there are minor differences, but overall they look very much alike."

Roxie was even more embarrassed that they had picked up on that detail about Brandon, but the resemblance was uncanny. "I know, Mom; that's why I dated him. There were major differences between Devon and Brandon that broke us up." Roxie was hoping they would let it go at that and thankfully they did.

After finishing their meal they all got up to leave, but as they were walking out Roxie had to pass the table that Brandon and the other suits were sitting at. She didn't want things to end on bad terms so she said to him, "Bye Brandon."

He didn't look at her as she walked past, but as she was about to walk out the door, a hand grabbed her arm just above the elbow and stopped her.

"Wait, Roxie. I'm sorry. Look I just want to start over so please rethink about moving back to Oklahoma. Stay in New York," Brandon said

"I can't do that Brandon," Roxie said feeling uncomfortable because she knew her parents were standing a few feet away from her listening to them.

"Why?" Brandon asked, becoming exasperated with her.

"Because I'm getting married."

"What?" At this he let go of her arm, stepped back and said angrily, "I see."

"Brandon there's no reason for you to be angry. We're not together anymore."

"Well I am angry. You weren't even dating anybody three days ago when you were still in New York and now you're engaged. This is bull." Brandon was drawing stares. The angrier he got, the louder he became. Then she noticed her dad about to step in so she knew she needed to get away from Brandon and end the conversation.

Turning, she started to walk away, but was stopped by Brandon's hand on her arm. Within seconds her dad stepped in and said, "Let her go or you'll find yourself with a few broken fingers young man."

Brandon looked from Roxie to her father. He saw a man that could easily give him a good fight, but realized that he needed to let his anger go for the moment. He released Roxie's arm and said, "This isn't over Roxie."

Roxie lifted her chin and stared defiantly at Brandon.

"Yes, it is," she said. With that, she turned and walked away with her father following her to the car and her mother walking beside her. Finally getting in her parents' truck she relaxed as she leaned back in the soft leather and avoided looking out the window knowing he would still be standing there.

A few minutes later her father pulled up in front of the hotel and she got out. She leaned inside the passenger side window and gave her mom a hug.

"Sorry about our dinner being ruined by that."

"It's all right. Are you sure you'll be all right until your flight in the morning?" her mother asked. Roxie stepped away from the truck.

"Of course I'll be fine. Brandon would never hurt me." Roxie was almost positive, but she had never seen him as angry as he was tonight at the restaurant.

"Okay, we'll expect to see you in a week." Waving goodbye, her parents pulled away and she went in the hotel and up to her room to try to get some sleep before her early day started.

Early the next morning, Roxie grabbed her bags and pulled closed the door to her hotel room. She was thinking of Devon and their upcoming wedding and was oblivious to her surroundings, only paying enough attention to make it to the elevator and get to the lobby on time so she didn't miss the shuttle to the airport.

Looking up to glance ahead, she finally noticed the man coming towards her in the narrow hallway and did a double take. "What are you doing here?" Roxie asked perplexed.

A deep voice answered her by saying oddly, "I'm here for you."

Roxie was never given a chance. He was standing so close to her that he grabbed her and spun her around with an arm around her throat and his other hand on her mouth to muffle her screams as he dragged her to the stairway.

He kicked open the stairway door, which was only a few feet from where they were standing, and shoved her through. As she spun towards her attacker, he slammed into her face with his fist. The pain was excruciating and then everything went black.

As Roxie slumped to the floor, he picked her up and made his way down to the parking garage. He was glad she had picked such an early flight. It would make being seen by any witnesses less likely.

He chuckled a little crazily as he carried her down the flight of stairs and said to himself, "I'm going to have fun with you."

Chapter 13

The pounding was so loud that Roxie couldn't understand why nobody was answering the door. Then she realized it wasn't someone knocking on a door, but was in fact a pounding in her head. She tried to roll over and cover her head with a pillow to block out the pain, but couldn't move her arms.

She was so groggy that trying to open her eyes was excruciating. It was better if she just let the blackness take her over. She would give anything to get rid of the pain.

He watched from the corner of the room making sure she hadn't woken fully and, after some fitful tossing, she settled down and went still. When she woke she needed to be completely awake for what he needed her to do. He hadn't thought to change his plans this way, but she was engaged to him now, it just couldn't be helped. He would use her to cause as much pain as possible for Devon Baxter before he killed them both.

He knew she wouldn't be awake for a long while and still he sat in silence. He couldn't help rubbing his knuckles. He'd hit her really hard and was still feeling the aftereffect. He got up from his seat and glanced at her one more time before walking up the stairs and turning out the single light in the room, pitching the space into complete darkness.

If he didn't drive her into madness with his plan, then staying any length of time in that black hole would help move things along.

Now what to have for dinner; maybe he'd go to town for pizza, but he wasn't really in the mood to be around other people. Oh well, he'd just dig something up in the kitchen. He momentarily forgot about his little prisoner. Besides, it wasn't like she was any kind of threat.

Whistling, he made his away across the yard to the house he currently had rented; he wasn't worried about anybody finding her. Nobody knew him here. It was unlikely that visitors would descend on a dangerous looking man living alone. If that did happen, it would be their own stupidity.

Painful light was piercing her eyelids and she was so thirsty that her throat felt like cotton candy. She hated cotton candy. At least she thought she hated cotton candy, her mind was so fuzzy she couldn't think straight.

"Wakey wakey," A deep voice crooned in her ear.

"What do you want?" she croaked the words past her dry throat.

"Well my dear, Roxie. I need you to make a phone call for me."

She got her eyes open only to see the silhouette of a man standing over the bed she was laying on. With the light behind him he was completely cast in shadows. She didn't understand what was going on. "I'm sorry, but who is Roxie and where am I?"

"Don't play games with me. You're Roxie Lancaster and you're engaged to Devon Baxter." Shaking her head at the information, she tried her best to remember anything. Nothing was making sense. "My head hurts so bad; I honestly don't know what you're talking about. Can I have a drink of water?" He said her name was Roxie, so that's what she would call herself. She didn't know what else to do.

He was watching her like she was the one that had hit him over the head with something. He moved over to a small table, which was the only other furniture in the dank, chilly room besides a chair and the bed she was on. Picking up a water glass and filling it from the pitcher, he came to the bed and leaned down to prop her head up and let her drink what she could before talking to her again. He was puzzled by her reaction. She wasn't hysterical about being kidnapped, but could possibly just not realize the situation yet because of how hard he had hit her.

Roxie, the name sounded familiar, but she had such a headache that she just couldn't think. She knew when she wasn't hurting quite so bad she would realize how much trouble she was in. After all, she knew enough to know she was in a dark room tied to a bed with a strange man standing over her. However strange he was she couldn't shake the feeling as she drifted back to sleep just how familiar he seemed to her.

Damn if the woman wasn't playing then she most likely had amnesia from the blow to her head. Just great. He had it all planned and now his bait couldn't remember her own darned name, but on the other hand she didn't recognize him either, which didn't really matter because she wouldn't see the outside of this cellar anytime soon.

After two more hours of her sleeping he got tired of waiting for her to wake up so he decided to take matters into his own hands. He picked up the water pitcher that was half full. It had enough in it to do what he needed.

Standing over the bed he watched her sleep for a few seconds; she really was beautiful; maybe not drop dead gorgeous, but definitely someone you would stop and look at twice. From her Honey colored hair to her lightly tanned skin and athletic body, she filled his heart with longing. But however he admired the face and body of the woman in front of him, she was just a stepping-stone.

Throwing the water in her face he watched as she jerked and started sputtering and pulling at the bonds that had her hands imprisoned. "What the heck?" she said, while she shook the water out of her face.

She could feel the goose bumps forming on her skin. The room was chilly before, now it was downright frosty. Looking up, Roxie was finally alert enough to realize the predicament she was in, but for the life of her could not remember how or why she was here. She just knew someone or something had hit her really hard and she knew the man responsible was staring down at her.

"Do you still not remember anything?" he asked, disbelieving.

Useless to fight, but feeling panicked that she couldn't get up she was trying to think of way out. "Only what you told me. Can you let me up?"

"So you really want me to believe you don't remember anything?" He watched her expression for sincerity.

"Look, I'm really freaking out here and see no reason to lie about not remembering something that you might want to know. So why don't you just tell me why you have me tied to a bed in a cellar and we'll start from there." She was yelling by the time she was done, but he seemed unconcerned by her raised voice. It wasn't like anyone would hear her.

"Okay, I'll believe you for now, but if you've lied to me that will only make what happens to you even worse. I am not someone you play games with." Even though he kept his tone light, the seriousness behind his voice bothered her more than anything.

Starting to shiver from the cold and the fact that the top of her shirt was wet from the water, she asked him, "Can I at least have a blanket? I can't help you with whatever it is that you need if I die of pneumonia."

"I suppose." Without saying anything else he turned and left the cellar by the staircase. Thankfully he had left the light on, but he didn't really promise to bring her a blanket and she was afraid to push for anything to eat. She didn't want him to figure it was more trouble to keep her alive by having to bring her things.

She was struggling to recall even one ounce of memory, but it was as if she had no past and that scared her. Her head still ached, but nothing like what it had earlier. She knew what he said about her being engaged was true because she could feel a ring on her ring finger, unless she was already married to this Devon person, but he wouldn't of had any way of knowing she had lost her memory so he would have no reason to lie to her. She was so confused.

Now that she was more awake she realized how exhausted she really was. She pushed the feeling aside, afraid to go back to sleep. Later, much later, she didn't know how many hours or if it had only been minutes that had passed, she heard the cellar door creak open and then a shadow fall down the stairs telling her it was daylight outside.

She watched him come down the stairs carrying, thankfully, a fleece blanket and a cell phone. Watching him warily from her position, she couldn't help feeling very vulnerable. She hoped he wouldn't pick up on it.

"Here, this should keep you warm enough," he said gruffly.

"What's your name?" Even though she couldn't recall anything, it wouldn't stop her from trying to learn something about him that might help her somehow.

"It's not important. If you had your memory you might say you recognized me."

So he was somebody that she knew or was familiar with. That was why he didn't seem like a stranger to her even though he had kidnapped her for some reason.

So she truly didn't recognize him or she would have thrown a bigger fit than she had. Interesting, very interesting.

"So why are you keeping me here?" Roxie was afraid of what she might hear, but needed to know what was in store for her.

"Well I won't bore you with all the details. I will tell you that I'm going to hold you for a few more days and then have you make a phone call for me." He knew that would confuse her.

"A phone call? That's it and then I can go?" Roxie was hoping that was all, but knew it couldn't be that simple.

Chuckling, he said, "I didn't say I would let you go, only that I would hold you a few more days. Think of it as you'll know when it's your time to die when I ask you to make the phone call for me."

Roxie felt all of the blood drain out of her face. She could barely breathe and had trouble getting out her next question.

"Why? What have I done to deserve this?"

"Nothing but become engaged to the wrong man at the wrong time." He turned and started back up the stairs tuning out the hysterical crying behind him. He left her until she either passed out again or until she calmed down enough for him to talk to her further.

A few days later Devon was pacing his office restlessly. He hadn't heard from Roxie since she had left three days ago and even though they had not made any agreement to keep in touch during the week, he couldn't help but feel panicked. He could call her cell, but he didn't want to make her feel as if he was checking up on her.

Lost in his thoughts, it was a few seconds before he realized the phone was ringing. Walking back to his desk and picking up his cell he looked at the caller ID hoping it was Roxie. It wasn't.

"Hello Lou."

"Devon, have you heard from Roxie?" Lou asked gruffly.

Lou's call made Devon feel his fears were ungrounded, but also made him feel extremely uneasy because she obviously hadn't contacted her parents either.

"No, I was just thinking of her though and wondering why she hasn't contacted anybody. I know she's only been gone three days, but still."

"Well her mother and I were going to call her but wanted to make sure she hadn't called you first," Lou said.

"I didn't want her thinking I was checking up on her and didn't trust her," Devon said while running his hand through his thick hair making it look unruly, but he could care less.

"Maybe you're right, but if I don't hear from her soon we'll call her and let you know, unless you hear from her first," Lou said.

They both agreed that was the best thing to do. Soon the conversation switched to ranching and the fact that Devon's cattle still hadn't been found or Wicks' murderer. Eventually Devon hung up the phone, feeling more alone than ever.

Devon continued pacing, not knowing what he was going to do. He had the worst feeling that something terrible was going to happen... he just didn't know what yet.

It had been four days since Roxie had been kidnapped and she dreaded every time she heard the door to the cellar open because she was afraid that would be the last day of her life. More than anything she obsessed over the fact that it would be pitiful if she died the last four days as her only memory. As she was caught in thought, her worst nightmare came true. She heard him coming down the stairs and strained to see if he carried a phone with him or not.

He did.

Smiling as he walked towards the bed, he said, "It's time."

Starting to cry, Roxie tried to plead with him one last time before he made her go through with this.

"Please don't kill me. I won't make the call." She hoped by threatening him she could gain some leverage, but apparently you couldn't reason with a psychopath.

"I'll just kill you anyway, but if you'll calm down I will not get rid of you immediately. I've found I still need you even after you make this call for me." He paused to let it sink in that he would keep her alive for the time being and then asked, "Agreed?"

Not answering immediately, Roxie took in a deep breath. She knew that was the only compromise she might get and she could only hope that she could figure out a way to get out of here before he could carry out his threat of killing her.

Letting out a pent up breath she said, "Agreed, but I would ask for a shower please. Just a shower and a chance to get up longer than the amount of time you give me to go to the bathroom." She prayed that he would grant this simple request. She truly was going quietly mad being in this cellar for days on end with only the filth to smell and the gray wall to stare at.

"After you make the call then I'll compromise with you, but don't try anything stupid because, believe me, if you think I've been toying with you so far it will be nothing compared to what I am capable of. Understand?"

She nodded, telling him without words that she understood.

"Who will I be calling and what am I supposed to say?"

Studying her for several minutes, he explained who he wanted her to call and why and hoped that her memory loss wouldn't cause any ripples in his plans.

After explaining everything to her, he let her right hand go from its bond so that she could grip the phone easily. He dialed the number for her and held it out to her as it rang on the other end.

"Here; do it just like we discussed and no tricks."

Roxie's hands were shaking furiously at the thought of calling a man she knew she was supposed to marry, but couldn't remember. She dreaded the thought of hurting him, of hurting anyone, but she couldn't see any other way out of this.

Hearing a man's voice come on the phone she asked, "Devon please."

"Roxie, thank god. We've been so worried. When are you coming home, Honey?"

Hearing the sincerity in the voice on the phone she started crying and glanced over at the man in the room with her and tried valiantly to swallow her tears and go on.

"Honey, what's wrong?" Devon asked.

"Umm Devon, I'm not coming home. I've decided to stay in New York."

"I don't und--" Devon started to say, but before he could finish his sentence the line went dead just like his love for her.

Chapter 14

"There. Take your stupid phone and shove it. I made your call, now what are you going to do?" Roxie was trying desperately to keep her wits, but she was afraid she was going to panic, begging him not to kill her.

Watching him watch her was unnerving. He hadn't so much as said a word after the call had been made. Finally quirking one side of his mouth in a semblance of a smirk, he shook his head and without saying anything, got up and left.

But of course he hadn't forgotten to retie her hand, which she had hoped to make him mad enough to leave and not remember, but apparently this man left no details unnoticed.

Her chest was still heaving and she could feel her body come off an adrenaline rush. She wasn't sure if it was from the fact that she thought she'd lived her last moment on earth or realizing she'd been given a reprieve from the maniac.

She wished that she could remember who she was and where she had come from. More than that, she wished she knew what purpose she had in his plans. She had tried several times in the last week, at least she thought it had been a week, to remember, but to no avail. She had lost all track of time. Anyway, she'd tried to get information from him on who he was and what he wanted, but the only thing he would allow her to call him was Buddy.

Eternal Peace

She snorted at the irony of it; she wasn't stupid enough to believe that Buddy was his real name and they definitely were not "buddies" together in this scheme, as his fake identity suggested.

She needed to get out of here. She knew the longer she stayed it would become even more impossible to get away because Buddy, she thought sarcastically, wasn't giving her enough food to help keep a rat alive much less a human being.

Maybe that was his plan all along. He would starve her to death tied to this damn place, staring at the ceiling. She had counted its cracks on more times than she cared to admit, only because Buddy left the light on during the day. It was the only way she could discern roughly how much time she had been trapped.

Closing her eyes briefly against the harsh glare of the light bulb hanging from the ceiling, Roxie shuddered. As much as she hated the dark at night, it was a thousand times worse during the daytime when she knew everyone was out enjoying the day. Her body was so stiff from being in one position. It was doubtful that that jerk would hold up his promise of letting her take a shower, which they had agreed on before the phone call; a hot shower would be absolute bliss right then.

Roxie tried to focus on something else. She was simply making herself depressed thinking too much of her situation. She had no immediate plan to rectify her problem, so she instead reflected on her abductor. She never got a good look at his face, but what she could see of it he seemed somehow familiar and he had implied that she knew him. If only she could remember.

He was a large man with thick muscles and was very tall, standing at least a few inches over six feet. What bothered her the most were his eyes; they were so dark, and when he was looking at her she couldn't tell their true color because of the light behind him as he stared down at her. His flat, emotionless eyes told her that the man didn't have a soul or even the least bit of compassion.

If she ever did get out of here at least she knew her name and the man she was to marry. Maybe she would have someplace to go and this Devon person could fill her in on her past since they were going to spend the rest of their lives together.

Devon's voice still sounded in her head. He had been so angry, but it hadn't been the anger that had bothered her as much as the sadness behind it. She wondered what this man was like.

Was he handsome? How long had they known each other? Was he kind and gentle with her? She wished she knew what kind of man he was because if he wasn't any of those things she would only be escaping one hell for another. She prayed she would remember. She had the most awful headaches each day, especially when she tried to recall any previous memories.

Finally falling into an exhausted sleep, her last thought was a prayer that she would make it out of this alive.

A week had passed since Devon had received the phone call from Roxie and he'd stayed drunk for most of it. He was such a fool to think that she would stay with him and marry him, but he still didn't understand it, not really. Surely it wasn't all a joke to her; breeze home for two days in the past eleven years, cause as much turmoil as she could and then leave town. During which had been two of the worst days of his life.

To make matters even worse, the cops still didn't have any leads on Wicks' murder or his missing cattle, but Devon didn't even care anymore. Right now all he worried about was if he had another bottle of Jack's in the liquor cabinet. Since he was lying on his couch, he wasn't really sure if it was worth getting up to go look for the bottle.

Giving up on the idea, he decided it would be better just to close his eyes for a few seconds.

Devon woke up several hours later to the phone ringing and, forgetting he was on the couch and not his bed, he rolled to the floor with a thud. Groaning from the impact of hitting the floor and knocking into the coffee table, he rolled to his knees, holding his head in his hands and feeling the bile rise up from his stomach. It burned his throat.

He tried to concentrate on taking deep breaths; after all, he couldn't concentrate on anything else, especially getting to the stupid phone. He heard his answering machine click on, followed by his recording. It was Milly Lancaster's voice leaving a message asking him to call her.

There was no way that he was calling Roxie's parents back; he didn't blame them for Roxie's defection, but he also didn't want to see anybody and talk about her either.

Now that the nausea was under control he figured he'd had enough self-pity for a while and hoped he could make it upstairs to his bathroom for a hot shower. As much as he didn't want to see or talk to anybody, he knew if he avoided Lou and Milly long enough they would come by to see if he was all right.

Groaning from having slept in one position for so long on a couch that wasn't long enough for a man his size, he made it to the door before he could feel his stomach rolling again from too much liquor and not enough food in the past week.

He just needed a hot shower pounding on his skin to help revive him and then maybe he could start facing the world again.

Roxie was so weak after two weeks of not having much to eat that she didn't think she could crawl her way to an escape if she wanted to. She never got a chance to shower. The only water she came in contact with was the little bit that Buddy provided her each day. It barely relieved her thirst.

Even though she couldn't remember if she was religious, she knew beyond a doubt that if she was to make it out of here she was going to pray for a miracle. She just hoped she didn't have to wait long because she doubted she had much time left.

She wondered if anybody was missing her. The only other person that Buddy had told her about was this Devon Baxter and she was pretty sure she had ruined the relationship that she had had with him.

What about her parents, a job, friends? Maybe dying would be more bearable if she remembered having anybody that cared for her. Maybe it was better this way. If she did have somebody that cared about her, maybe it was better for him or her to be left in the dark; she didn't want to worry anybody and have him or her wonder what had happened to her.

Letting out a shallow breath (breathing was even becoming too hard anymore) she tried not to cry. She just needed to rest and closed her eyes.

It was close to midnight as he watched the house and cellar. Luckily there was some light from the moon casting an eerie glow over the surrounding area. Watching the place had become his nightly ritual; he knew something or someone was being held in the cellar and his curiosity always got the better of him. It was why he always got into trouble wherever he went.

Knowing that the man renting the house had left a little while ago, made him want to check the cellar all the more, but he didn't want to get caught.

Taking any precaution he could, he'd parked his old Chevy truck a distance away in the woods and made sure it was camouflaged enough so that it wouldn't be readily visible from the road. Checking back towards the drive way once more to make sure it was clear and double checking to see if he still had his flash light, he started making his way across the ground to the underground cellar that was a short distance from the dark house.

Trying not to make any sudden moves, he approached the doors slowly and noticed that they weren't locked, which was strange because if you had something you wanted not to get out it seemed you'd lock the doors at least.

Wiping sweat from his face with the sleeve of his jacket that was starting to cool anyway from the chilly January night air, he glanced over his shoulder once more before taking the door handle and pulling up with all his strength to open it. He wasn't prepared for how heavy the door was. He lost his grip and the door fell the opposite direction and banged against the ground causing enough noise that he was thankful nobody was in the house to hear it.

With shaking fingers, he grabbed for the flashlight that was tucked in his back pocket of his jeans. He turned it on and shone it down the entrance, but only the stairs leading down into the earth were visible.

Taking a deep breath, he took the first few steps down and stumbled, catching himself on the wall. He got the distinct impression that he was walking into a grave, but shook the notion off. He was simply walking down into a cellar below ground, a very deep cellar.

As he got closer to the bottom he couldn't help but feel that he wasn't alone. Suddenly he thought this hadn't been one of his best ideas. He was about to turn around when he heard a moan followed by a whispery voice that said, "Help me, please." All thoughts flew straight out of his head as he turned to race back up the way he had come, thinking that maybe he'd stumbled upon a grave after all and there was a ghost somewhere in the inky darkness.

Halfway back up the stairs he stopped and realized that this was why he had come... to see what was down there and obviously it wasn't a grave, but a cellar. Although the voice had been faint, it was still very much human; at least he hoped.

Closing his eyes for a second, he turned to go back down the stairs once again. This time he reached the bottom and took his flashlight out to scan the interior. For a moment he thought he was going crazy. It was empty. Then he saw the body that had called out to him with the faint voice and nearly threw up from what he saw.

It was woman that had slowly been starved to death. Her wrists were bloody and raw from the ropes keeping her secured to the bed. That was why the doors hadn't been locked; whoever had put her here didn't fear her getting away, but didn't figure on anybody coming down here either. Plus she was filthy and smelled, he noticed as he slowly approached her. Hating to see anything suffer, he sat on the edge of the mattress and dug his pocketknife out and tackled the bonds on her wrists.

"Lady, can you walk?" After his shock had worn off, he realized that he needed to get them both out here before the strange man came back and found the cellar door open. He wasn't sure if he was strong enough to lift her and carry her all the way back to his truck.

Moaning, Roxie turned her head and saw him sitting beside her on the bed. She was too weak to defend herself if she needed to and it was pitch black in the small room with the exception of his flashlight. Fighting her way from the fog her mind was in, she realized he had freed her wrists, but she was too weak to move them. Hearing his question, she knew it was pointless to answer him; she just didn't care if she lived anymore.

"I'm getting you out of here, I promise, but we need to move fast before he gets back." There wasn't anything he could do but try to carry her out of here and hope he made it to the top of the stairs and back to his truck in time.

He no longer bothered to ask her any more questions. By the look of things if she didn't get medical attention quick she wouldn't last much longer anyway. Bending over her, he placed his hands under her and picked her up. Still holding his flashlight, he directed the light towards the stairs and made it to the top before he took a break. Even though he could tell she'd lost a considerable amount of weight from her imprisonment, he wasn't used to carrying a hundred plus pounds of dead weight around.

After twenty minutes of exhausting walking and some jogging he finally made it back to his truck. He knew that whoever had kept her would know that she was gone by the time he came home by the open cellar door. There wasn't much time. Making a quick decision, he got her into the cab and left as soon as he could.

Realizing that the woman was falling asleep, he shook her shoulder to keep her awake as he raced her to the hospital. He wanted to have any information he could get before she passed out. Something he could tell the doctors, a name at least.

Trying to lift her eyelids to see who was talking to her, Roxie tried to focus on the person sitting across from her in the cab of the truck. "Yes," she said.

"I'm Rick; what's your name?" Rick said

"Roxie Lancaster... at least I think so," she said

"You're not sure?" he asked. How did she not even know who she was? He was about to ask another question when he caught the last name she had given. He wondered if she was related to the Lancasters that owned a ranch on the outside of Peace.

"I can't remember anything. I only think that's my name because that's what he told me after he kidnapped me," Roxie said, hoping that this man would keep helping her.

"I know of a place that's owned by some Lancasters. It's a ranch not too far from here, but I'm taking you to the hospital right now and let the police handle the rest," Rick said, worriedly.

"No, he would find me. Please, the man that held me also told me that I was engaged to a man named Devon Baxter. Do you know anybody by that name?" Roxie asked hopefully.

Surprised to hear Devon Baxter's name, Rick nodded immediately. Devon Baxter owned the ranch that supplied rodeo stock to all the major rodeos in the country. It was also one of the places that Rick was hoping to hire on at. "Yes, his place is next to the Lancaster place. I was hoping to get a job there on the weekends."

Thinking it was odd for someone to want a job just for the weekend, Roxie looked at Rick more carefully. He now looked a lot younger than he had originally.

"How old are you exactly?" she asked. With it being the middle of the night it was almost impossible for her to focus. She was surprised when he answered.

"Seventeen," Rick said. "Look I think since I know where Mr. Baxter's place is and the fact you're engaged to him that I should take you to his house since you don't want to go to a hospital."

"Fine. I don't care as long as that man doesn't find me again and I need to warn this Devon Baxter," Roxie said as she drifted to sleep slumped over the seat with her head resting on the console.

Luckily he wasn't far from the town of Peace. He could drive through and make his way to the ranch and still be home, hopefully, before his parents realized he was gone. He promised himself that the next time he got the lecture from his parents about his curiosity that he would listen because he never wanted to be in this situation again.

It was going on two o'clock in the morning and Devon couldn't sleep; he was trying real hard not to pick up the bottle lying next to him and drinking himself into oblivion. So, instead he was pacing a hole in the rug that was in the living room until the memory hit him of Roxie on that very same rug the first day she had been back and they had been together before her parents had walked in on them.

Cursing, Devon left the living room as fast as he could and went to his office. Maybe some book-work would help keep him focused; he did have a ranch to run after all.

After several minutes of fruitless attempts at trying to balance a set of numbers on some invoices, he gave up and dropped his head in his hands before running his hands through his slightly long hair. Frustrated with himself, he leaned back in his chair and closed his eyes, but kept seeing her face every time he did. He didn't think he could handle this twice. He'd made it eleven years without her; surely he could do it again. It didn't make sense why would she make that big speech about how much she loved him and had only wanted him to show the same feelings if she was just going to leave him anyhow. Slapping his hands down on his desk he got his answer, she wanted him to come after her. She wanted him to follow her to New York and bring her back.

At least that's what he hoped was the case. He sure didn't relish making a trip only to find she had duped him again. Making up his mind he turned to his computer on his desk and made travel arrangements that would take him to New York later that morning, just a few hours away. Feeling better than he had in days, Devon was just walking up his stairs to go pack when he thought he heard a vehicle come up his driveway, but shrugged the notion away. Living in the country meant that sounds always carried.

Reaching the top of the stairs, he heard the doorbell and was surprised that anybody would be out this late. Huffing a breath because he really wanted to pack and catch some sleep if he could before he had to leave, Devon hurried back down the stairs.

By the time he'd reached the front door, he realized that whoever was there was leaving. He heard the vehicle peel away from his house and back down the road. He shrugged to himself and didn't bother looking out. Turning back, he headed back up the stairs to take care of everything. He had only three hours to pack and catch some shuteye. He didn't need to leave any later than five in the morning to make his flight to the city.

Roxie tried to roll over on her side and get up from the porch where Rick had left her. At least that was where she had woken up. He had at least left a blanket with her, but she was so weak that she could barely get her arms under her, much less support any of her own weight. Giving up she pulled what she could of the blanket on top of her and closed her eyes. She was still so exhausted that she didn't mind the hard porch underneath her and the fact that she was outside on a very cold night.

At four fifty five Devon was on his way down the stairs with his suitcase and a newly found sense of determination. He was wide-awake even though he'd had less than three hours sleep last night. He still couldn't help but wonder who had come to his house a few hours ago.

Going to the side door off the kitchen because his truck was parked on that side of the house, he went through the door and walked to his truck, throwing his bags into the back. Opening the door he climbed into the cab realizing he should've came out earlier and warmed his truck up. Oh well it wouldn't take long for it to get toasty.

Backing out of his spot beside the house, he came even with the front porch and noticed a pile of cloth or rags on his front porch. Wondering what they were, he put the truck in park and climbed out annoyed at this point because he was going to be late if he procrastinated much longer.

Walking around to the front of the porch and up the three stairs, he immediately realized it wasn't a bunch of rags, but someone bundled in a blanket. Shaking the person, he hoped to the good lord above that whoever it was wasn't dead; he couldn't handle another dead body on his place, not on top of everything else that was going on.

Turning the body over on its back he realized it was a very rank individual; then his heart stopped as he realized it was not only a woman, but was Roxie. When he saw her wrists he knew that she'd been somewhere terrible.

"Roxie, wake up Honey," Devon said. When she didn't stir, he felt for a pulse after seeing how cold she was. After several frantic seconds of not feeling one, he finally felt a faint pulse under his fingertips. Holding her tight, he picked her up and was starting down the stairs to his pickup to take her to the hospital when he looked down and saw her open her eyes a fraction.

"It's okay Honey. I'll take care of you, I just need--" Devon was cut off when she started crying and he was stunned when she said faintly, "Please don't put me back in the cellar."

Roxie had woken enough to recognize the features of the man who was holding her. Even though her vision was bleary from her own tears she knew that this was the same man that had kidnapped her.

Her fate was sealed.

Chapter 15

Devon was reeling from first finding Roxie almost half dead on his porch to hearing what she had said about a putting her back in a cellar. First priority would be to get her to a hospital. Gently lifting her into his pickup, he laid her down on the full backseat. Since it was a crew cab, it had plenty of room for a person to lie down and be relatively comfortable for a short ride.

As he was adjusting the blanket over her, he noticed the dried blood on her wrists and hands. He could feel himself filling with rage, knowing immediately that he was capable of murder for whoever had done this to her.

Finally getting her situated (thankfully she'd passed out again), Devon started the truck and began to pull out the driveway quickly. He didn't like to think what pain she might be in from injuries that he couldn't see. He drove for the hospital as fast as he could, pulling his cell phone out of his pocket as he concentrated on not killing them both with his driving.

He placed the first call to Lou and Milly. He felt guilty now that he was sober that he hadn't returned any of their calls until now.

Trying to dial their number proved more challenging than he had thought with his driving and he realized worst of all that his hands were shaking badly, which he knew wasn't from the lack of liquor, but rather from finding Roxie in her condition so unexpectedly. Finally getting the number punched in, he waited to hear the phone start ringing and waited several tense seconds while somebody came to it and answered.

It was slightly past five in the morning when the phone beside Lou and Milly's bed started ringing; they were usually both early risers, but with the strain of the past week they were both exhausted. Staying up late and worrying about their daughter not to mention their worry for Devon was becoming too much for both of them. Not only had they not heard from Roxie and her reasoning for not coming home, but also the fact that Devon wouldn't answer any calls from them had been taking its toll. "Answer the phone, Lou," Milly said as she rolled over to her side. Then she sat straight up and pushed Lou in the shoulder when he didn't move fast enough. "Lou, get the phone it's on your side, it may be Roxie."

Lou leaned up on his elbow, reaching for the phone. He hated to disillusion his wife by telling her that Roxie probably wouldn't be calling them anytime soon. "All right just a second, Honey."

Picking up the phone, he answered it right before the answering machine clicked on he said, "Hello." Then he heard Devon's voice on the line and knew something was wrong from how bad his voice was shaking.

"Lou, there's no time to talk, but you and Milly need to meet me at the hospital," Devon said taking a breath to steady his nerves; it didn't help.

Hearing the anxiety in Devon's voice, Lou got up and started pulling his clothes on from last night.

"What's wrong Devon? Are you hurt?" Lou asked anxiously. From the corner of his eye he could see Milly changing out of her nightclothes and into some jeans and a sweatshirt. She hastily pulled her sneakers on, not bothering to tie them. He turned his back to her so that he could find out what was wrong without seeing the worry in her eyes.

"It's Roxie that's hurt, not me. Just hurry. I'm taking her to Peace County Hospital," Devon said. "I've got to go. I need to call the sheriff." Then he hung up without waiting for a reply.

Lou quickly chucked the phone behind him and it landed on the bed. He turned to Milly.

"We need to go now to the hospital." Lou didn't want to tell her anything more until they were in the truck. He knew she would get too upset to concentrate.

"What's wrong Lou? You're scaring me," Milly said, worry evident in her voice.

"I'll explain on the way. We need to go now," Lou said, pushing her out the door.

Grabbing their jackets from the wall hanger by the back door, they hurried out into the cool morning, both racing to the pickup. Climbing in, Milly turned to Lou and said, huffing a breath from their race out of the house, "Tell me what's going on, no stalling."

Running a hand through his hair to show his agitation, he looked sideways at her and said, "Devon was the one that called and he said that we needed to get to the hospital quick; he didn't have time to explain."

"Has Devon been hurt?" Milly asked. Besides her daughter, Devon was like her own child. Then the blood froze in her veins when Lou looked at her and shook his head no.

Afraid to ask but needing to know Milly said, "Roxie?"

When Lou nodded his head in confirmation, Milly started crying.

"I don't understand. She's supposed to be in New York. How did Devon know she's hurt and we didn't?" Milly sniffed into a Kleenex; she'd had the habit of keeping them in her pocket these days.

"I don't know, Honey. He didn't give me any details, just said we needed to get to Peace County Hospital. Beyond that we'll have to find out when we get there. Believe me, Devon will answer all our questions," Lou said anxiously.

Half an hour later they pulled into the parking lot of the hospital and raced into the emergency entrance searching for Devon. Not seeing him immediately, they approached the nurse's station.

The slightly plump nurse was looking down at some paperwork, but upon hearing them stop at the counter she looked up and asked, "Can I help you?"

Lou and Milly were still looking anxiously around, but tried to focus on the nurse.

"Our neighbor, Devon Baxter, called about our daughter, Roxie Lancaster. Can you tell me where either one of them are?" Lou asked.

Upon hearing the names, compassion entered the eyes of the nurse and she said, "Yes sir. If you'll follow me I'll show you to a private waiting room. Then I'll let the doctor know you've arrived."

"Can't you give us any information, please?" Milly asked. She was close to breaking down again if somebody didn't give her some answers.

"I'd rather wait and show you to the waiting room. Mr. Baxter can explain everything until the doctor can see you," said the nurse.

Given no other choice, they followed her to the waiting room. Upon seeing the door, they rushed past her and were met by a grim faced Devon. He was staring at the opposite wall, acting as if he hadn't heard them enter the room.

Approaching Devon cautiously, Milly laid a hand on his shoulder making her jump when he jumped, surprise written on his face when he realized he was no longer alone. The nurse discreetly left not wanting to bother any of them.

"What's going on son?" Lou asked. He felt helpless.

Devon looked at one and then the other. He choked on his words because he didn't think he could get out what he needed to tell them. Finally taking a deep breath he said, "I found Roxie on my front porch this morning; she's in pretty bad shape."

After hearing this both Lou and Milly slid into the seats opposite Devon in the waiting room and said simultaneously "How?"

Devon put his head in his hands and shook his head back and forth saying, "I don't know. The only thing I figure is I heard a vehicle last night, about two in the morning, and someone rang the doorbell, but by the time I reached the front door someone was already pulling away from the house. I didn't think it was important so I went back upstairs without looking outside. Now I know that Roxie must have been dumped off on my porch, but I never looked outside and I didn't leave the house until a few minutes before five this morning when I noticed the bundle on my porch. She must have been there for three hours in the cold while I slept inside," he said, his voice ending on a whisper. He was not able to look at her parents in the eye after the way he'd ignored them the past week and now he'd probably killed their daughter.

Seeing the look of guilt on Devon's face, Lou said, "Devon you can't blame yourself for anything that has happened to Roxie; it's not your fault." Seeing Devon shake his head at what he said, Lou continued.

"We'll talk about this later, but what's wrong with Roxie? We need to know what to expect."

Remembering back to when he had found her, he blocked it out and concentrated on her parents. He told them, "She's extremely malnourished and she has some really bad raw areas around both her wrists and ankles from being tied up. That's all I know. I brought her here as fast as I could and called you and the sheriff on the drive here. As soon as I checked her in they took her into a room and starting working on her and I haven't heard anything on her condition yet. I'm still waiting on the doctor."

Taking it all in, Milly started softly crying into her husband's shoulder. She couldn't say anything; she was too stunned.

Lou just held his wife for what seemed hours. Finally, when they didn't think they could wait any longer, the door opened and they rose, but were deflated to see it was only the sheriff.

Devon was the first to speak, saying angrily, "Where the heck have you been? I called your office hours ago."

Putting up both his hands as if to ward off any attack he thought might be coming Sheriff Carter said, "I'm sorry, but I had another emergency that I was on before your call; there was no help for it. Please except my apologies." Seeing the tension leave Devon's body he then asked, "I'm going to need a statement from you, Devon, about what happened."

"Sit down. I've already filled them in on the story," Devon said motioning with his hand toward Lou and Milly before taking his seat.

Devon began his story again. There wasn't much to tell since he still didn't know himself what had happened to Roxie. After telling the sheriff the story, nobody said anything for several minutes.

"So you didn't see the vehicle at all?" the sheriff said, writing something in his little book as he spoke.

"No, it was full night outside. I only heard the vehicle and the doorbell. The next thing I knew, the vehicle was leaving before I had ever reached the door," Devon stated.

"So why didn't you look outside? With everything that has happened lately, I would think you'd want to know who was near your place," the sheriff asked.

Exasperated, Devon realized that he was going to have to reveal the part of the story he hadn't told anybody. "Because I wasn't thinking clearly."

Interest peaked over this comment, the sheriff asked again, "Why?"

Looking over at Lou and Milly, knowing that they wanted an answer to the question also, Devon answered finally, "Because I'd just made travel plans for New York."

"Wait a minute, I don't understand. Why were you going to New York?"

Seeing that he had stunned Roxie's parents with the news, he said, "Because I was going after Roxie to bring her back."

Even more confused, the sheriff looked at each face before asking, "Okay the last I knew, Roxie had just come home after eleven years of being gone. You're telling me that after a little over two days she goes back to New York suddenly, especially after already agreeing to become your wife? What am I missing here?"

Devon looked him in the eye before telling the next part and then said, "The morning you were at my house, well after you left, Roxie told all of us that she was leaving for New York, but only to take care of any loose ends she had so that she could move back here and we could be married."

"Nobody thought to tell me she was leaving? A murder had been committed on your ranch, Mr. Baxter," the sheriff said angrily.

They all looked at Sheriff Carter with surprise and then Devon said angrily, "You can't believe that she would have anything to do with what happened to Todd Wicks?"

"I don't know, but I do find it odd that she shows up out of the blue and leaves just as quickly." He knew he was treading on dangerous ground, but he was the sheriff and he needed answers. It was necessary that he ask these questions; it didn't matter that he truly didn't think she had anything to do with the murder or the cattle being missing.

"Go to hell," Devon said, anger raging through him. "Roxie may have been gone all these years, but I've known her since we were kids. We grew up together. She would never do something like this."

"I think you'd better leave now." Lou said in a low voice. He was standing dangerously still with his arm around Milly; she was his anchor right then because all he wanted to do was fly across the room and slam his fist into the sheriff's pompous face.

"Look, as unpleasant as all this is, I need to stay and hear what the doc says about all this so that I can write up my full report," Sheriff Carter said cautiously. Then he stated, "Look, I don't think she had anything to do with it, but a man was murdered on your property and whoever did it may have been the one to kidnap her thinking she saw him. I don't know exactly what's happened here, but we need to find out and fast before someone else is hurt."

Realizing that he finally neutralized the tense situation, he continued, "Also, I'm curious to know how she got away. Somebody must have helped her I don't think the guy would have just dumped her on your front porch, seeing as she's the only person that could help us identify him. Find him or her then maybe we can find out whose behind all this."

"Did you remember her saying anything else besides the reference to the cellar, which won't help us at this point. With this being Oklahoma, every house has a cellar because of tornado season."

"No, I barely heard her say that... her voice was so faint," Devon said. He was racking his brain again for anything that might help them and then he remembered the phone call. He just then realized that she had been put up to it.

As realization struck, Devon's spine snapped at attention and he began swearing. "I should have guessed, but I was so wrapped up."

Milly, hearing the anxiety in his voice, raised her head up from her husband's shoulder and asked, "What is it Devon?"

Devon looked at her and then Lou and visibly swallowed before saying, "I'm sorry. I just didn't think of it before."

"What, Devon?" Sheriff Carter said, scooting forward till he was seated on the edge of his seat, waiting expectantly for what Devon would say next. He had his little book flipped open, ready to take notes if necessary.

"The phone call about a week ago, remember Lou? I told you Roxie called and said she wasn't coming back."

"Yes, but what does that have to do with this?" Lou asked.

"I think she was put up to it. The phone call was so brief and I could tell she'd been crying, but I thought it was to the fact that she was calling me to tell me the news of not coming back. Maybe it was because she had been kidnapped and this person put her up to it," Devon said knowing with each word he said it was truth.

"But why?" Milly asked, thinking she was missing something.

The sheriff answered before Devon could say anything more.

"Because whoever kidnapped her wanted all of you, but especially Devon, to think the worst of her so that no one would think to look for her. If that was a week ago then she's most likely been held for the past two weeks because no one's called from New York expecting her, she never made it there."

Shocked silence met the sheriff's words; he took the words right out of Devon's mouth.

Milly started crying all over again with Lou trying to comfort her.

"It will be all right," he said. "Everything will work out fine."

Milly started shaking her head and said with tears in her eyes, "We don't know that. For the past week we've all thought the worst of her. The whole time my baby has been a prisoner somewhere."

Devon closed his eyes and let the guilt washed over him, he hadn't even thought of that until Milly put it into words. Thinking back on his last week of self-pity, he knew that he would never, for as long as he lived, get over the feeling of guilt.

Finally, after having waited most of the morning for any news, the door to the waiting room opened and the doctor came through, looking weary. This was the worst part of being a doctor. He hated facing the family and having to deliver news. It was even harder with people he knew. He'd known the Lancasters and Baxters for years. He had even delivered both Roxie and Devon.

Sensing it wasn't good news, Devon asked the question that nobody wanted answered. "Is she going to be all right Doctor Samson?"

Not answering right away, Doctor Samson went to the seat next to Milly and sat down. He took her hand in his and finally answered, looking into both their faces and back at Devon.

"Its obvious that Roxie's been severely neglected for an extensive amount of time and her wounds around her wrists and ankles had become infected."

Pausing and wanting to phrase his next words carefully, the doctor continued.

"She was so weak when she came in that it was a wonder really that she's lasted this long. Roxie did, however, slip away once on us." Hearing everybody starting to get upset, he hastily added, "We were able to bring her back, but barely."

With too much emotion clogging his throat, Devon stared at the doctor and asked, "Will she make it?"

"Honestly, I don't know. At this point it's touch and go. She was barely breathing on her own after we revived her and we had to put her on life support. My recommendation right now is that all of you spend as much time with her in the next twenty four hours; prepare yourselves for the worst."

Turning to the sheriff the doctor asked, "Do you know who did this to her?"

"No, we were hoping she could tell us something about who dropped her off on Devon's porch," the sheriff stated.

"I see." The doctor turned back to Roxie's parents; he knew this would be the hardest part of the discussion. "I need both of you to sign a waiver with the understanding that if Roxie doesn't come back to us and continues to need life support, then after a certain amount of time that we let her go."

Milly started sobbing. Lou's eyes were suspiciously bright with unshed tears. Finally he asked, "You really think it's necessary to talk about this now?"

"Unfortunately yes. She got medical attention so late that I'm not sure she'll make it very long. Even though that's all true, miracles do happen. So pray and visit your daughter. However, you needed to know all of this so that each one of you are prepared to say your goodbyes to her when the time comes."

Coming to his feet, he motioned to the sheriff to follow him outside the room to give them all time alone. As they were almost to the door, a nurse burst in out of breath saying anxiously, "Doctor Samson we need you in Roxie Lancaster's room immediately."

Breaking into a run, Doctor Samson fled from the room and down the hallway. Calls of "code blue", loud beeps and yelling echoed throughout the area as the doctors and nurses tried desperately to revive Roxie Lancaster.

Then everyone within hearing distance of the waiting room heard the denial that was ripped through a man's throat as he yelled and then sadness invaded all their hearts as they heard Devon weeping because he feared above all else that he had just lost his soul mate.

Chapter 16

Roxie surprised everyone by surviving another week, proving that miracles do happen. Devon knew that he had prayed more in the last week than he'd prayed in his whole life. During that time someone had contacted the FBI on what was going on in the small town of Peace, OK. Devon was tired of the endless questions that just went round and round. No results came of any of it.

He'd stayed by Roxie's bedside tirelessly. He would only return home to pick up a change of clothes and grab a shower, in which case Roxie's parents sat with her. Sitting in Roxie's private hospital room, Devon continued to hold her hand. There'd been no change in her condition. Looking at her face, he grimaced at what he saw. Her face was still extremely thin, but showing signs of renewed health from all of the nutrition that the medical staff was giving, even though it was purely liquids. Thankfully they'd treated the abrasions on her wrists and ankles in time to kill any of the infections that were starting.

Something that nobody had seen right away were the yellowish bruises that were now starting to fade. Upon closer inspection, it looked as if someone had hit her in the face to make her cooperate.

Devon hoped that he never had to experience the amount of anguish that he'd felt when the nurse had said they couldn't revive her a second time; he didn't know what she was holding onto for survival. Somewhere inside of him he hoped it was him that she was hanging on for. He remembered someone telling him that talking to her would help, so he started each day with her telling her a story from their childhood, hoping to hear her laugh with him, but knowing it was fruitless to expect it.

The story he chose today was about tree climbing. When they were ten years old, they had both wanted to see who the best tree climber was. Since both had claimed to be the best, an argument and challenge ensued. Devon spoke quietly, seating himself in a chair next to Roxie's bed and looking down at her hand as he traced circles its back absently.

He kept his voice steady and strong as he spoke. "I still remember the day. It was a beautiful spring day and it was finally warm enough for us to stay outside all day. We got into an argument about who could climb the big oak behind your house the fastest. Next thing I knew, you pushed me to the ground and headed around your house to the back yard." Chuckling, Devon paused before continuing, "I was mad that a girl thought she could push me into the dirt and then claim to climb a tree better than me so I set out after you to prove you wrong. I mean you crushed my ego and I needed to defend it."

Roxie became aware of a steady voice talking to her before she managed to get her eyelids open enough to focus on a face. What she saw was the most gorgeous man in her life. He had thick dark hair and a strong masculine face that was looking down at her hand. He was tracing circles on the back of her hand and it gave her shivers. She couldn't see his eyes, but knew by looking at the rest of him that they would be just as spectacular. Finally she heard the story he was telling to her and realized he was talking about the two of them as children. Not wanting to alert him that she was awake, she waited until the end of the story.

"So," Devon continued. "We both made it to the tree, but no matter how fearless you always seemed, you also had a fear of heights and started to back out. Even though my pride had been bruised, I tried to be gallant. That's hard to do when you're ten years old, but I took your hand gave it a squeeze and asked if it would help if we went up together." Devon took a breath remembering that day as if it was yesterday. "You were still trying to be brave and you looked at me with your big eyes and said quite sternly for a little girl, 'If I wanted your help, Devon Baxter, I'd ask for it.' Then you turned with your back ramrod straight and walked away. You never did climb that tree."

Roxie realized that this was the man that she was supposed to marry. His story seemed so familiar to her, and it should, since it was obviously their childhood. He still hadn't looked up. Something about the profile of his face was familiar and yet so disturbing. It was imperative that she saw his eyes.

Not being able to talk because of the breathing tube down her throat, she squeezed her fingers around his hand to get his attention.

Devon went so still when he felt her fingers move that for a second he thought it was his imagination; then his heart started pounding in his chest and when he turned his emerald green eyes in her direction, he felt his breath actually stop as he looked into her face. She was awake and looking at him with a mixture of disbelief. Oddly enough relief came into her eyes.

Roxie could feel her fear drifting way the second she saw Devon's green eyes. She knew that this was not the man who had kidnapped her. Immediately, Devon's presence made her feel safe.

However, the man that had held her captive must still be a relative of Devon's. There just couldn't be that many men with same eyes and strong handsome facial features as the one sitting next to her.

She also knew by the relief and anxiety in Devon's face that she must have worried him a great deal. He looked bone weary. She just wished she knew something about him other than the fact that they were to be married; she knew before today was over that she would hurt him again by her memory loss.

After several stunned minutes of looking into Roxie's eyes, Devon jumped into action. He began running for the door and yelling down the corridor for Doctor Samson to get there quick. Not bothering to wait, Devon turned back to the woman in the hospital bed and sank gratefully back down in his seat.

As soon as Devon opened his mouth to speak, nurses were running into the room with Doctor Samson trailing behind them. They pushed Devon aside and told him to wait outside.

Not listening to them, but moving to the front of the room, Devon watched them examine Roxie. Soon, the doctor turned in Devon's direction and said, "Devon why don't you wait outside until I've had a chance to give Roxie an examination?"

"No, I'm staying."

"It wasn't a request. Wait outside," Doctor Samson repeated. Seeing a protest forming, the doctor tried another tact. "Please leave Devon. Go and call Roxie's parents."

Bowing his head a minute, and then looking at Roxie who was looking anxious, Devon knew that Lou and Milly should be here for their daughter so he left the room without another word.

Striding towards the exit of the building, Devon was pulling his cell phone from his pocket when he glanced up and saw both Lou and Milly coming towards him. Seeing him at the same time, cell phone in hand and grin on his face, Milly and Lou were hopeful. "By the grin I'm hoping its good news about Roxie," Milly said.

Taking her hand Devon smiled at her and said, "Yes, she's awake."

Lou hugged his wife and said with relief, "Thank God. Did she say anything?"

Devon shook his head.

"Not yet; the breathing tube is still in her throat. The doctor asked me to leave so that he could examine her. I was just about to call you guys."

Feeling an eerie sensation on the back of his neck, Devon felt like they were being watched. It was crazy because there were plenty of people around them, but the feeling just didn't seem to go away. He looked over his left shoulder. All he could see was someone around the corner, but it looked like a doctor. The man was wearing a white coat. Shaking his head at his own foolishness, he concentrated on Roxie's parents.

"Come on; there are some chairs we can sit on outside Roxie's room." Devon got on the other side of Milly and they all walked back down the hall to wait.

The man weaved through the hospital hallways as if he actually was a doctor. No one seemed to notice him. *Well, well... so she is going to live*, he thought as he left the hospital. And as long as she didn't have her memory back he might just let her live a little longer. At least long enough to watch Devon Baxter die a horrible death... just like his foreman.

It wasn't like he had anything to worry about. The kid that rescued her wouldn't be talking anytime soon. He'd learned a final lesson about snooping on other people's property. He had made sure that the kid had told no one. They were all fools. There was nothing any of them could do to prevent the inevitable. They couldn't stop a threat that they didn't know was coming.

He still had one complication to take care, but all in good time.

"Okay Roxie, I'm going to unhook the breathing tube and remove it from your throat. It will be extremely uncomfortable, but it won't take more than a second. Blink if you understand," said the doctor. Then, seeing her blink, he directed the nurse to turn the machine off as soon as he removed the tube, allowing her to breathe on her own.

After the tube was disconnected there was a whooshing sound of air being released, and he gently tugged on the tube to dislodge it. Roxie started gagging, but finally it slipped free leaving her gasping for air on her own.

Eternal Peace

"Do not speak. Give yourself a few minutes to acclimate and then only whisper," the doctor said. "There are some mighty anxious people who want to see you." Turning towards the door, he was stopped by a hand holding onto his arm.

Looking down he noticed her agitation and asked, "What's wrong?"

"Who?" Roxie whispered, feeling her throat was so raw she could barely get the words out. She brought her hand up to her throat to caress the outside in an effort to soothe it, but felt nothing would help with the rawness.

Perplexed he said, "Your parents of course and your fiancé, Devon."

"Don't remember," she rasped out.

"What don't you remember?" he said, worry lacing his words.

"My life," she said. Her voice was becoming stronger as she talked.

Knowing that her family would have to wait, he sat down on the edge of her bed and said, "You don't remember anything?"

Rubbing her throat again she replied, "Only from the time that I woke already kidnapped." Pausing she continued, "The man that held me only told me my name and the name of the man I was to marry."

"Judging by the bruise on the side of your face when you came in over a week ago, you must have taken a pretty good knock to your head. That must have been the cause of your memory loss," the doctor said. Sighing, he added, "I will explain to your parents and Devon before they see you. However, they are extremely anxious to see you. Are you up to it?"

Nodding she said, "I think so."

Patting her hand he stood up to leave, but was once again stopped when she asked, "Will I get my memory back?"

"I don't know. We'll need to do a CAT scan, but normally time will tell one way or another. Right now you need time and rest to recover physically."

Opening the door to her room, he saw her parents and Devon rise out of their chairs, but with a wave of his hands he motioned for them to sit back down. This was not news he wanted to deliver while they were standing.

Watching the doctor's face as he exited Roxie's room, Devon knew that there was something wrong and he was afraid to find out what.

"How is she? Can we see her?" Devon asked before anybody else could say anything.

"She's awake and able to talk, however, she needs to take it slow," the doctor began.

Devon could sense something wasn't quite right. "What aren't you telling us?" he asked.

"She's suffered memory loss. The bruise that was on the side of her face seems to have caused some head trauma. We'll know more after a CAT scan is done."

Lou spoke up.

"How much memory loss, exactly?"

"I honestly don't know how severe it is; it's lasted from the time she was kidnapped to now, so it could take a while for her to regain her memory... if at all."

Devon felt his world crashing down around him again.

"Does she remember anything at all?" he asked.

"No, except from the time she woke up after being taken."

"So she won't know any of us or our names?" Milly asked, finally speaking up after the shock of hearing this news wore off.

"She only knows the names the kidnapper gave her, which is her own and yours, Devon. She also knows that she was supposed to marry you, but as far as actually knowing any of you goes, she's blank."

"Will she see us?" Lou asked. Devon had wanted to ask, but was afraid to hear the answer.

"Yes. I've asked her to see all of you because I know how anxious you all are to finally see her. She seemed all right with the idea. However, not too long because she is still exhausted and she'll need her rest."

Roxie found herself picking at the blanket covering her. She was becoming increasingly nervous about seeing people that she couldn't remember. She didn't want to hurt anybody's feelings by saying or doing the wrong thing. Oddly enough, she didn't think she was going to have a problem with Devon Baxter. The story she'd caught him telling to her was soothing and she felt safe being around him.

She thought that as long as he was in the room everything would be okay, but she didn't really know what kind of relationship they'd shared before her memory loss. She figured if they had known each other as kids and were going to be married that she could trust him, hopefully. Hearing the door open, she pushed herself up to a sitting position and tried to give a smile. Unfortunately, it felt more like a grimace because every muscle in her body was stiff, including the ones in her face.

In walked a couple; she assumed they were her parents judging by their age. The woman was an older version of herself. Roxie knew this because the nurse had helped her to the restroom where she saw her face in the mirror. Roxie could feel her heart start to pound in worry when she saw the kindness and worry in her parents' eyes as they studied her. It made her feel less tense in their presence.

"Mom, Dad?"

Milly started sniffing.

"You remember?" she asked, hope shining in her eyes.

"No, I'm sorry. I didn't mean to imply that I did, it's just that the doctor said he would be sending you all in to see me," Roxie said nervously.

"Oh, of course," Milly said, hope diminishing.

Looking from one face to another and last at Devon, Roxie realized that he was restraining himself from coming to her side and she felt sympathy for him. Oddly wanting to offer him comfort, she held her hand out to him. Surprise came over his face and he stepped forward silently and enfolded her hand with his.

"You gave us all a scare," Devon said with a deep sigh.

"I'm sorry that I don't remember any of you, but somehow you all seem familiar to me," she said. She knew the moment that the words left her lips that she was speaking the truth.

Roxie was starting to speak again when the door to her room came open and there stood man that also seemed familiar to her. He wasn't as gorgeous as Devon, but he was certainly striking. He was carrying a bouquet of flowers that were just as stunning as he was; even though he seemed familiar, she also sensed a feeling of foreboding in the air.

Still holding Devon's hand, Roxie kept quiet. Assuming that either Devon or her parents knew this strange man, she waited for an explanation. It became immediately apparent that Devon had no idea who the man was.

"This is a private room, buddy. Meaning family only," Devon said, not bothering to be sociable; he disliked the stranger on site.

"I think Roxie will welcome me," the stranger said just as coolly. He didn't remove his eyes from Devon's piercing stare.

"Why is that?" Devon said becoming tense as he stared the other man down.

"I'm Brandon," he said. He paused for a moment and a smile spread across his striking features. "I'm Roxie's boyfriend from New York and just who the hell are you?"

Chapter 17

Devon started to step away from Roxie's bed to show him just exactly who he was, but was forestalled by Roxie's hand holding on to his firmly. He was angry that Roxie might have a boyfriend that she hadn't told him about, but as he looked back at her, he saw the pleading and confusion. It made him stop and realize that it was time to protect her and to stop jumping to conclusions, especially now when she needed him the most.

"I asked who you are, Cowboy," Brandon sneered.

Before Devon could speak this time, Lou stepped forward between the two men and said angrily, "Don't concern yourself with who he is. You're not welcome here."

"Why don't you let Roxie tell me she doesn't want me here?" Brandon said. He was confident that she wouldn't turn him away, especially if she wanted to keep her reputation intact in the business world.

Stepping closer to Brandon, Lou said in a low voice, "My daughter is in no condition for your kind of company so why don't we step into the hall so I can explain; then I expect you to leave peacefully."

Brandon stared at the older man for several seconds before making the decision that, although he wasn't going to back down, it might be the wisest choice to leave for now and come back when she had less company or none at all, then he could make her see reason. He didn't like to lose.

Dipping his head a fraction, he acknowledged that he would do what was asked of him, but there wasn't any reason she couldn't have the flowers that he'd brought. Stepping around Lou and holding the bouquet in front of him, he placed them on the table across the room and left silently.

As Brandon had stepped forward to leave the flowers, Devon had felt Roxie stiffen and wondered if she remembered something about this man that made her uncomfortable, but he didn't want to ask while Brandon was still in the room so he waited. As soon as Lou and Brandon stepped out into the hall, Devon turned towards Roxie and, not letting go of her hand, he asked, "Do you remember him, Honey?"

She honestly wasn't sure. She thought about it a moment before answering, but it was all still so unclear.

"No, there's just something about him that makes me uncomfortable. I can't explain it. It's probably completely irrational."

Devon knew she was struggling, but was relieved that she hadn't remembered Brandon. Deep inside he selfishly hoped that if she were going to remember anything, it would be himself.

"It's okay, Honey. Don't worry. Your memory will come back," Devon said.

Devon was about to offer Roxie a cup of water when he heard Milly clear her throat. They both turned to look at her.

"Do you want me to explain to you who Brandon is?" she asked.

Both Devon and Roxie looked at one another in surprise and then Devon asked, "You know who he is? Is that why Lou said the bit about him not being welcome?"

Nodding her head, Milly said, "Unfortunately, besides us, Brandon was one of the last people to see Roxie before we dropped her at her hotel the evening before her flight to New York."

"Who was he to me?" Roxie demanded. She hated that she couldn't remember on her own.

Devon could barely wait for Milly's answer, but he tried to remain patient for Roxie's sake. She was clearly having enough trouble remembering things without him causing a scene. Who was this Brandon? And how was he important enough in Roxie's life to visit her in a hospital in Oklahoma? New York was a long way away.

"Brandon is your co-worker… mostly," Milly said evasively.

Devon picked up on her tone and looked at her with eyes that said 'well, go ahead.' She sighed and continued.

"Well, Roxie, you did date him," Milly said. When she saw the anger in Devon's eyes she hastily added, "But not anymore. Apparently you two split a couple of years ago." After this statement she saw Devon relax again and hoped that they could drop the subject.

"So what he implied about us dating was a lie?" Roxie asked anxiously. She hoped that she hadn't been a person that was engaged to one man and dating another. If that's what she had been like then she didn't want to remember her old life.

"Yes, I'm very sure of it. The way you acted towards him in the restaurant, well, it was definitely over for you. Brandon, however, wanted you back and said as much at the table that evening. He was very angry with you and confronted you again when we left the restaurant that night," Milly said.

Devon, hearing this all for the first time, tried to hold his temper.

"Did you or Lou tell the Feds about this?" he asked.

"Well no. I didn't think of it at the time," she said. "Do you think we should? I mean he was angry at the time and definitely rude here a minute ago, but do you think he would have anything to do with Roxie's kidnapping?"

Devon didn't know, but he wasn't above telling the Feds about Brandon even if it was just to check him out. If it caused the guy problems, well he was a jerk anyway and needed to be taught a lesson. As he was thinking this, the door opened and Lou came back inside.

Quickly, Devon ran through the idea with Lou about alerting the Feds about Brandon to have him checked out. Lou was about to agree when Roxie spoke up.

"You guys are forgetting something."

They all turned to look at her questionably and she continued. "I saw the guy that took me and I can describe him. It wasn't Brandon."

With the excitement of Roxie coming to and Brandon's unexpected arrival, nobody had asked Roxie about her kidnapper, the circumstances or most importantly who had dropped her off on Devon's porch.

"Who was it Roxie? Can you tell us about him?" Devon asked. The last thing he wanted was to sound pushy, but he would do anything to catch this guy before he hurt anybody else.

Roxie paused for a long moment. She wanted to be sure that she chose her words very carefully to avoid offending him, but he needed to know everything.

"It's strange," she said.

Confused by her answer, Devon looked over his shoulder and her parents, but they only shrugged their shoulders and continued to wait Roxie out.

"What's strange?" Devon finally asked.

"The resemblance between the two of you," Roxie said.

"Do you mean the similarities between Devon and Brandon?" Milly asked.

Hearing this Devon realized that the other man had looked a great deal like him, but he knew Roxie was referring to her kidnapper. For some reason it sent a cold chill down his spine.

"Although that resemblance is weird, I think Roxie was referring to the similarities between her kidnapper and Devon. Am I right, Roxie?" Lou asked quietly.

Roxie kept her eyes focused on Devon throughout the exchange.

"Please don't take offense. Even though I don't remember you or us, I feel completely safe with you," she told him. He could see the truth behind her eyes and relief washed over him. He waited for the 'but' in her sentence that he knew was coming.

"But you also scare me some because of the resemblance. He looked almost exactly like you, only he was older, but he had the same black hair and green eyes. And your eyes show emotion; his didn't. They were flat like he had lost his soul or never had one."

Devon couldn't believe what he was hearing and was afraid to look at Lou or Milly for fear that they were thinking the same thing. Then Roxie only made it worse when she said: "He also had a slight scar on his left cheek."

Roxie stopped. She could sense the tension in the room and suddenly she was very much afraid that everyone knew who her kidnapper had been but her. Nervously, she removed her hand from Devon's and started picking at her blanket again. She finally asked, "Do you know who it is?"

Devon's mind was whirling. He had to think. There had to be a rational explanation, but he couldn't come up with one. Standing up and pacing, he started running his hand through his hair. He could feel the agitation building with no way to release it.

"You all know who it is don't you?" Roxie asked. She could feel her heart pounding through her hospital nightgown.

Seeing her daughter becoming upset, Milly came to rest a hand on Roxie's shoulder. She looked at Devon.

"You're scaring her. Both of you quit scowling at her; it's not her fault."

Both men stopped immediately. They hadn't realized that their actions were distressing Roxie so much.

Letting out a breath Devon said tightly (to no one in particular), "You just described my father, Roxie."

Then Devon thought back on the description she had given and said, "Except about the eyes; they're not emotionless. He may not show his emotions, but he's not soulless."

Roxie started crying. She couldn't help it. Maybe she'd been wrong, but the similarities were so uncanny. She madly brushed the tears away and was about to try to say anything to console Devon when Doctor Samson came in and immediately took in the situation.

"I need all of you out. Roxie needs her rest."

Once the small group had been ushered into the hallway by an accompanying nurse, the doctor closed the door behind them.

"Please don't come back until you can talk to her without upsetting her."

Milly opened her mouth to begin to explain to the doctor exactly what had been going on when Lou stopped her.

"We need to tell the authorities what she told us before anything else is done," he said in a low whisper so that only she could hear. "Doc, she's crying over something she told us and it upset us therefore upsetting her."

"Well, all right," the doctor said, beginning to relax. "But she still needs her rest and if you call anybody to come see her make sure they wait a few hours. She needs to sleep."

They all came to the bed one at a time while Roxie was still sniffling into a Kleenex and kissed her on the cheek saying they would be back later. The last to leave was Devon and, although he wanted to give her a real kiss, he decided it would be better to give a kiss on the cheek also, no point rushing her when she didn't remember him.

Squeezing her hand before leaving, Devon headed for the door with Roxie's eyes following his every move.

Roxie looked after Devon as he left and was disappointed that he had only gave her a kiss on the cheek. She barely knew him and she couldn't very well expect anything else from him especially after she'd just accused his father of kidnapping her.

She also wondered about the boy that had saved her, but then sleep claimed her. Her dreams were very disturbing.

Devon was pacing the corridor restlessly when he looked up and saw the Feds coming towards him. Roxie's parents had gone to the cafeteria for a bite to eat; they were afraid to all talk about what Roxie had revealed.

He'd been trying to reach his father for weeks, but to no avail. Now he hoped that the reason wasn't because his father had kidnapped Roxie or killed their foreman, Wicks. Nothing was making sense anymore.

The two agents that had been sent to investigate Roxie's disappearance were named Roberts and Hillman. Both men had shown up about the time Roxie had, which seemed weird because they'd never explained who had called their attention to what was going on in Peace.

Both agents wore nondescript clothes in an effort to not draw attention, but in a small town like Peace, they were bound to stick out a bit. Regardless, they always seemed to know what was going on around them. Agent Roberts was at least six three with blond hair and a muscular build; he could hold his own in a fight. Agent Hillman was a few inches shorter, but was no lightweight either and Devon wouldn't relish having to go up against either one of them, and definitely not both of them at the same time. They seemed to really care about what happened to Roxie, especially since they didn't really even know her, but Devon sensed that they also knew more than they were letting on.

"Any change, Mr. Baxter?" Agent Hillman asked.

So the doctor hasn't seen them yet to tell them the news, Devon thought. *I guess it falls to me.*

"Yes actually," he said.

Eternal Peace

Surprise showed on their faces and Agent Hillman said, "Why weren't we called?"

"Because it came as a surprise to all of us, including Roxie. She's been asleep for a few hours," Devon said impatiently. Honestly, he hadn't wanted to call them because he knew then that he'd have to tell them about his father and that he hadn't been in contact with him for over three weeks, not since the night of Wicks' murder. He prayed that call wasn't a coincidence.

"You still should have called us. We need to know of any changes immediately," Agent Roberts finally spoke in a controlled voice.

"Well you know now. By the way I have a question of my own," Devon said, stepping closer to both agents.

"What's that?" Hillman asked.

"Just how the hell did the FBI get involved in this case and where's the sheriff? Shouldn't you have notified him that you were coming to the hospital? You know, professional courtesy and all." Devon could hear the anger in his own voice, but he didn't bother apologizing. He was sick of people expecting him to jump through hoops when no one seemed to be capable of finding who did this to Roxie.

Both agents looked at one another before answering.

"We were tipped off."

"So what? People go missing all the time. Why was she so important to the Feds?"

"Ms. Lancaster is a very influential person in New York. People take notice when a millionaire investment banker takes a leave of absence and then disappears completely," Agent Roberts stated. "As for the sheriff... he'll be here eventually, I'm sure."

Devon looked from one to the other and sensed they were still holding something back, but knew he wouldn't get any more information out of them. Knowing there was no more time to stall he said, "You'll have to wait for her to wake up before she can tell you anything."

"Has she told you anything, Mr. Baxter, that will help us?" Roberts asked.

Devon paused, but didn't say anything right away.

"Look, if you don't tell us we'll only get it out of her when she's awake. We'll still get her statement, but the sooner we know something the faster we can find who did this to her. Maybe that person is somehow connected to your foreman's murder and the stolen cattle."

Closing his eyes a minute, he prayed he wasn't making a mistake, but everything was leading to his own father and the Feds would find out soon enough when they questioned Roxie. "She described her kidnapper to us," Devon said, finally feeling as if he'd betrayed everything that he knew in the world.

"Who is 'us' exactly?" Hillman asked, taking a notepad from his pocket and beginning to scrawl down notes.

"Lou and Milly Lancaster and myself; no one else."

"Go ahead," Hillman said

"She basically described him as my look-alike, only older and with emotionless eyes and a scar on his left cheek," Devon said, looking anywhere but at the agents. Maybe if he hadn't been looking away from them he would have caught the look they shared and the surprise that came and went on their faces, but they quickly masked this before Devon saw it.

"She described my father almost to a tee, except for the eyes. And, no, before you ask I truly don't believe he could be involved in this. He couldn't be," Devon said fervently

"When's the last time you saw your father?" Roberts asked.

"He left a few days after my mother's funeral, well over a month ago. I haven't seen him since." Devon hoped they wouldn't ask when the last time he'd actually talked to his father, but knew it was wishful thinking.

"Have you talked to your father since then?" Roberts asked.

Devon was frantically thinking of any way he wouldn't have to tell them about the phone call, but he knew that if they really wanted to know they could just obtain his phone records. He'd just lost his mother; he didn't want to be responsible for making his father a fugitive from the law.

"No stalling Mr. Baxter. When was the last time you talked to your father, John Baxter?" Roberts asked again.

"The night Todd Wicks was killed," Devon said, barely getting the words out.

"I see," Roberts said finally.

"We'll need a current picture of your father for identification as soon as possible," Hillman said.

"This doesn't make any sense. Why would my father have any reason to do any of this, especially steal cattle that are half his, kill his own foreman or kidnap Roxie, tell me that," Devon said angrily.

"We don't know why people do the things they do. We've captured some that had never had any brushes with the law and one day something snaps and they go on a killing spree. Look, if we find your father, all we want to do is question him. Have you tried getting in touch with him since that last contact?" Hillman said. He had clearly given this speech to many a family member in the same position.

Sitting down in the chair against the wall opposite Roxie's room, Devon said, "Yes, several times in last three weeks, but I haven't been able to get a hold of him. I've been worried because he promised he was coming home after I gave him the news of Wicks' murder."

"Okay Mr. Baxter. We understand this is tough for you. If you hear from your father let us know. We need to talk to Roxie's doctor at this point to see when a good time will be for us to talk to her," Roberts said, sensing the need to back off from questioning him any further at this point. They got what they'd needed anyway.

Turning to walk away, Agent Roberts paused and turned halfway back to Devon to ask one more question. "Do you by any chance know a boy named Rick Olden and his parents?" he asked

Devon looked up at the agent not understanding what a boy and his parents had to do with anything.

"No, Why?"

"They were found in their barn hanging upside down with their hands tied behind their backs; their throats had been cut." Pausing to see the reaction on Devon's face he continued. "Murdered just like your foreman. Whether it's your father or not we are now dealing with a serial killer," Roberts said before turning away once again to find the doctor. He didn't bother to hear any reply from Devon Baxter.

Chapter 18

As they made their way down the hallway of the hospital, both agents looked at one another.

"Go find the doctor," Roberts said. "We're going to need to make a phone call." Not bothering to see if he was obeyed or not, he turned and made his way to the exit, pulling his phone out at the same time.

Making his way outside, Roberts dialed the phone number he had memorized and waited for an answer.

"What?" a man answered tersely, not bothering with politeness.

"She's finally awake and she's describing you as her kidnapper," Roberts said in his usual brusque manner. "What do you want us to do, John?"

"Damn. I need more time to finish this and do the job as it was explained to you, nothing further," John Baxter replied.

"You don't have much time. I can only keep this quiet for so long, especially with the other murders. I'll have my boss on my ass asking for a report of progress before long," Roberts said getting worried about this whole situation.

"I'll handle your boss when the time comes, if it comes to that," John said. "Whatever happens, you best not reveal anything to my son before it's time. Leave that to me. If you don't, you will answer to me and you won't be able to hide behind your badge." John hung up the phone. He would let the agents think whatever they wanted to from what he had said. Maybe, if they became worried enough, he would step it up and cover himself a bit better. Cursing under his breath, Agent Roberts snapped his phone closed. He made his way back into the building to find his partner and the doctor for the update.

He was frustrated. When they'd been assigned to the case, they'd been given minimal information. Their only contact was John Baxter and their task was to find this Roxie Lancaster. Now she had resurfaced, and it was looking like John Baxter was becoming their prime suspect in her kidnapping.

What worried him most were the murders. The way those people had been killed disturbed him; only a truly sick individual could do that without leaving any evidence or motive behind, except for the Bar B foreman who could have been killed over the cattle. The kid and his parents were a different story; what the connection was, Roberts had no idea, but he was hoping for some clue to point him and his partner in the right direction. What they did know was that the same person had killed each victim; the whole stinking mess revolved around the Bar B Ranch and the Baxters.

Spying his partner and Doctor Samson by the nurse's station, he headed in their direction. They needed to talk to Roxie and get her entire story, and there was still the matter of her sudden reappearance and how she'd gotten away from her kidnapper.

As he approached he asked, "Doctor Samson, I hope you remember me from before. I'm Agent Roberts. When would we be able to speak with Ms. Lancaster?"

"As I was telling your partner here, as soon as she wakes up you're welcome to question her. You both need to be careful though, she's still extremely weak," the doctor said, looking from one agent to the other to make his point clear.

Nodding their agreement, they both turned to find the waiting room so they would not be overheard. The room was surprisingly empty when they arrived and Roberts quickly told Hillman about his phone call with John Baxter.

"I don't understand any of this. I just about croaked when Devon said Roxie described his father as the kidnapper," Agent Hillman said. He paused for a moment before continuing. "We should call the boss." With that, he pulled out his cell phone, but was forestalled by Roberts putting a hand over it.

"No, we leave things as they are," Agent Roberts said. "Let's talk to Roxie Lancaster first and get the story from her. We don't want any screw-ups on this case. Everything needs to be official for now."

Just then the door to the waiting room opened. A nurse told the men that Ms. Lancaster was awake and that they were welcome to see her, but to keep the visit to a maximum of twenty minutes. She would need to rest again.

With the nurse leading the way back down the corridor to Roxie's room, the agents spotted Devon and Roxie's parents sitting outside, also waiting for when they could see her again.

Both agents stopped in front of the small group. Agent Roberts said, "She's awake and we need to question her."

"Can we be with her?" Milly Lancaster asked.

"No, she needs no outside influence from anyone. We hope that she'll be able to shed some light on what's going on," Agent Hillman said.

Without letting anybody say another word, both agents turned and entered her room.

Upon entering the room they found Roxie propped up in her bed looking a little better from when they'd first seen her.

"Ms. Lancaster, I'm Agent Roberts and this is Agent Hillman; we're with the FBI. We need to ask you a few questions." Roxie offered a weak smile to them both and then held out her hand.

"Please call me Roxie."

"All right. Doctor Samson filled us in on your medical history and we understand that you've suffered amnesia?" Roberts asked.

"Yes. I don't remember anything prior to when I woke up in that cellar," Roxie said. She couldn't help remembering back to when she'd come fully awake and realized what had happened to her.

"Roxie, we'll get to your story from the beginning in a minute. Right now we're curious to find out how you escaped and ended up on Devon Baxter's front porch?" Roberts asked. Hillman was taking notes, not bothering to be the one asking questions. He preferred to observe and listen.

"Let me think." Roxie closed her eyes, trying to remember a night that was so fuzzy that she had been on the point of giving up. Opening her eyes and looking at the agents she said, "I remember a man coming down the stairs of the cellar with a flashlight. I called out to him for help."

"So a man helped you escape?" Roberts asked.

Shaking her head Roxie said, "No, a boy really. He said he was seventeen. His name, I believe, is Rick."

At the mention of the boy's name both agents became alert, darting glances at each other before Roxie realized something was wrong.

"What is it? Is he in some kind of trouble? He was very sweet and was only trying to help me."

Not bothering to answer her question right away, Roberts asked, "How did Rick come to find you there? Where was the man that had taken you and held you?"

"I don't know. Rick mentioned something once on the way to Devon's ranch about his curiosity, but I was in and out of it for most of the trip," Roxie said. "Tell me what you don't want me to know about him."

Letting out a breath, Roberts thought it best to finally fill Roxie in on everything from where she had come from to what had happened at Bar B Ranch and finally about the murder of Todd Wicks, the missing cattle and the entire back-story of her kidnapping.

As Agent Roberts told her the story, Roxie braced her head in her hands. She felt like her head was going to explode from the tremendous amount of information being thrown her way. Even though she didn't remember what he was telling her, she couldn't help feeling responsible and guilty. It was about to get even worse when Agent Roberts began to answer her previous question about Rick.

"The boy that helped you, do remember if his last name was Olden by any chance, Roxie?" Roberts asked. He knew the answer before he got it from her, but still needed to hear it from her all the same.

"I believe so; I mean, that sounds right to me. Please tell me what you know about him. I'd like to thank him," Roxie said looking at them both anxiously.

Roberts looked over at his partner before he answered.

"Rick Olden was killed along with his parents not long after you were rescued, at least no more than twenty four hours later."

Knowing that their time with her was almost up, both agents knew they didn't have long to get the story from her about her kidnapping and now she was in tears.

"Roxie, I know you're upset and terribly confused, but you need to concentrate for us just briefly, long enough to tell us what happened to you after you woke up in the cellar," Roberts said, coming around her bed until he'd reached the chair and sat down. He hoped that he was making himself less intimidating to her.

Sniffling, and trying to get her emotions under control, she wiped her nose on a Kleenex and started from the beginning.

After her story was over Agent Roberts mentally went through the story in his head quickly to determine if there were any holes, but she sound completely sincere in her recount of the experience. However, one thing did bother him, the motivation for the actual kidnapping.

"So from what you've told us the only thing the kidnapper used you for was the phone call he wanted you to make to Devon Baxter about you not returning from New York?"

Roxie nodded her head.

"Yes, perhaps it would have meant something more to me if I'd had my memory. I even got the feeling that he was somehow familiar to me, but maybe that's because he looks so much like Devon."

"One more question and then we'll leave and let you rest. Can you please describe your kidnapper to us?" Roberts asked. At the back of his mind he was hoping that there would be something different from what Devon had told them. If not, then the killer they were looking for would not only be Devon's father, but their contact on the case.

Roxie thought back to all the times in the two weeks that she'd been held and pictured him in her mind. She recalled the features as best as could and she was able to give the exact description she'd given earlier to Devon and her parents, but excluded Devon's fears about it being his father. She didn't want to be responsible for any more ruined lives if she could help it.

"Okay. You did good Roxie. We appreciate your cooperation. If you remember anything else, here's my card; just give me a call," Roberts said standing up.

"There is one more thing, Agent Roberts, and I don't know how much it will help, but I did ask his name. The only one he gave me was 'Buddy'," Roxie said, hoping that it would somehow help them in their search.

The name was useless, but it showed she was willing to give any and all information she had.

"Thanks," Roberts said. "We'll see what we can come up with."

Motioning towards his partner, they turned to leave. As they were about to close the door, they heard the bedside phone begin to ring. Both men paused for a moment to see if she'd answer it.

"What do you want?" Roxie said, holding the phone to her ear.

Seeing her face lose what little color it had, Agent Roberts looked at her questionably and she pointed at the phone with a shaky finger and mouthed 'kidnapper.' Incredulous and astounded that the man had that much brass to call the hospital, Agent Roberts mouthed to Roxie, "Keep the conversation going."

Nodding her head that she understood even though she was terrified, Roxie gripped the phone and tried to concentrate. There wasn't anything the man could say that she wanted to hear anyway, but she was hoping this would help catch the guy.

"I just wanted to make sure you hadn't forgotten me," the maniac stated.

Darting a glance at the agents Roxie took a fortifying breath and said, "How could I forget such evil-hearted lunatic as yourself?"

Ignoring the question the voice replied, "Do you think you're safe just because you're surrounded by the FBI?"

"Why'd you kill that boy and his family? Why did you kill Todd Wicks?"

"They got in my way," the voice replied. It was hard to understand him from the distortion, but there was a cruelty in his voice nonetheless. "Also you can tell the agents in your room, good luck."

Feeling cold chills creep up her spine, Roxie almost threw the phone away from her before asking her next question, "How do you know there are agents in my room?"

At her question, both agents snapped to attention and moved away from direct contact of the hospital window. They took up posts to the sides so they could both look out onto the parking lot. They frantically scanned the area, but saw no one suspicious. Regardless, they weren't about to let their guard down for a second.

"Because I'm watching you."

With that Roxie heard the line disconnect and tears silently slipped from the corners of eyes as she tried to hold onto what little composure she had.

Trying to get a hold of herself, she slipped the phone back in its cradle and saw Agent Roberts speaking quietly, but urgently into his phone before ending the call and slipping it back into his pocket.

"He said he was watching me," Roxie said with a wobbly voice, "Did you get a trace on him? I assume that's why you wanted me to keep the conversation going."

Making sure the curtains were closed this time before moving away from the wall, the agents glanced at one another.

As always Roberts was the speaker of the two, "No. It wasn't long enough, but we've got people scanning the immediate area right now for him." Even though he wouldn't say it to her, he knew the man would be too smart to be caught out in the open such as the hospital parking lot.

"So what happens now?" Roxie asked, leaning her head back against her pillows feeling utterly exhausted.

"You'll need around the clock protection. Agent Hillman will make sure that you have a guard placed at your door immediately. We need to take every precaution; he'll be coming for you sooner or later to finish what he started. To him you're nothing more than a loose end," Roberts said before turning to leave. He needed to talk to Devon Baxter about his father.

Chapter 19

Devon was weary to his very soul and wished this nightmare would end. He rubbed his hand around the back of his neck in an attempt to relieve the tension in his muscles. It was pointless. Nothing was going to relieve the stress until they found the man responsible for all of this. Devon had been at the hospital so much that he knew the staff by name and he didn't want to; he knew that was horrible, but he just didn't care anymore. All he wanted in life was to marry Roxie and have a family, but darn he'd been dealt some life altering blows lately. It honestly was making him question everything that was real in his life.

Yesterday he'd been so ecstatic when Roxie woke up. It seemed like she was finally on the mend, except for the problem with her memory, which was only one more obstacle between the two of them. Then after the two FBI agents had questioned her, there'd been a phone call made to Roxie's room. Now all visitors that even neared Roxie's room had to be screened by local law enforcement. He was glad she was being protected, but it was a constant reminder of everything that was going on. The police had told Devon about the call made to Roxie and whom they thought had made it. Because of it they were seriously looking towards his father as primary suspect in everything that had happened lately, especially the murders.

They'd drilled him for hours yesterday evening about his father. Where'd he go after his wife's funeral? How long as he been gone exactly? When's the last time you tried to call him?

The questions went on and on until he was very much afraid that exhaustion would finally do him in, but thankfully they stopped. They still did not look satisfied, but he truly didn't have much to tell them. Their persistent questioning made him seriously doubt everything he knew, especially when it came to his father. Had there been signs after his mom had died that might of clued him in? If it were his father, then why would he steal their cattle from their own ranch?

Devon's questions were going round and round in his head until he felt he was going to get a pounding headache. Then there been the boy the agents had asked him about. Devon hadn't a clue about how this boy connected to anything until the agents filled him in on the gory details. This poor boy had been the one who had saved Roxie, and he had died for it.

No matter how many times he circled the facts, there was also a part of him, down deep in his gut, that couldn't and wouldn't believe that his father was the bad guy in this. There must be some explanation.

Agents Roberts had asked one question that had surprised Devon and that was if his father had any siblings or possibly a twin brother.

Devon told the agents that, like himself, John Baxter was an only child. He knew this with certainty because his mom, Lilly, had completed a family tree for her family side and his dad's side of the family; there were no relatives even alive on the Baxter side anymore except for John and Devon.

It was a new day and he'd been here all night, having promised Lou and Milly that he would stay even though there was a guard posted around the clock at Roxie's hospital room. They'd both been exhausted and needed some time to go home and recuperate themselves, but had promised that they'd be back around noon.

Glancing at his watch, Devon noted that it was almost ten now. He thought he'd given Roxie enough time this morning to ensure she got enough sleep. After everything that had happened, he still wanted to make her his for the rest of his life; he just wished she could remember him. If she couldn't, he would have to let her get to know him all over again, even if that meant telling her every childhood story and what information she'd given him about her time away from home all those years, he would do it. Man, he was tired and wished he could curl up his bed and sleep even if it was only a couple of hours.

Getting up from his waiting room chair, he went to her.

Roxie was propped up in bed having just showered with some assistance from a nurse. She was also bone weary, but mainly it was from lying in bed so much. She passed the time by watching it rain; it'd been raining all morning and from the weather report she'd watched earlier it probably wouldn't stop for a while.

It was just one of those days that a person should be home, curled up in front of a fire with a good book or a lover. With that thought Roxie snorted and then giggled. Thanks to her memory loss, she didn't know if she had either a good book or a good lover.

With a slight smile on her face, she didn't hear the door to her room open until a shadow fell across her bed and startled her. She jumped and placed her hand over heart when she realized it was Devon.

"I'm sorry. I didn't mean to scare you; I just wasn't sure if you were awake or not," Devon said, noticing how much twenty-four hours had done for her. Except for the yellowish bruise still adorning the fair skin of her face, she looked well on the way to recovery.

Roxie kept her hand placed over heart. It was still racing, but not from the fear of the startle. Devon was an attractive man. Every time she saw him she couldn't help it. Her heart always skipped a beat. She couldn't believe that she was truly engaged to him. She also couldn't believe how truly gorgeous his eyes were. Upon first glance they were a deep green, but if she looked really close she could see that he had the tiniest flecks of gold around the irises that were almost invisible; she imagined they would disappear when he got angry, making his eyes go soft to hard instantly. Then she wondered what other parts of him would go soft to hard instantly, not realizing she was looking at him from head to toe stopping at his groin for far too long.

Devon felt like he'd just climbed a mountain. Desire had hit him so fast that he was almost out of breath from it. It was all because Roxie was eyeing him like he was a piece of candy she wanted to unwrap. He didn't know what had gotten into her, but suddenly he felt that she wouldn't have such a problem with getting to know him again. Frankly she didn't look like she would mind if he climbed into bed with her, but he thought better of it since she was still obviously weak and they were in a hospital.

Chuckling Devon asked her, "Like what you see?"

Blushing Roxie raised her eyes. Oh geez, had she really been staring at his package? Maybe she could claim another bout of amnesia in the next two seconds to hide her embarrassment. Oh well, maybe the truth would throw him off. Looking him straight in the eyes this time, and fighting a giggle, she said, "Yeah I do."

Devon's eyebrows rose at her honesty. She sounded just like the old Roxie. It threw him for a minute before reality came back to bite him. "You don't remember anything, do you Honey?" he asked hopefully.

Regretful, Roxie lowered her eyes and shook her head no, but it had felt nice to be called Honey by him. He had such a gentle voice, but she wouldn't tell him that. She'd inflicted enough embarrassment on herself for one day.

Feeling disappointment all the way to his toes, Devon said, "Well it was too good to be true that you would wake up and remember our past."

"I'm sorry Devon. Believe me, I want more than anything to remember my life and especially what we mean to each other," Roxie said shyly, looking down at the blanket covering her.

Sighing, Devon took the chair next to her bed and sat down.

"You're going to pick that blanket to death if you don't quit," Devon said. He was amused that she seemed to be shy around him. He had to remember that this wasn't the Roxie he knew. Picking up her hand, he started stroking it just like he'd done when she was unconscious for so long.

Trying not to be nervous, Roxie looked at Devon and knew it wouldn't be hard to love this man. There was just something about him that made her feel safe. She knew she would never be able to explain why.

Seeing the frown that suddenly made his mouth downturn, Roxie became worried.

"What's wrong, Devon?"

"Roxie, I need to know that if it was my father that kidnapped you... I want you to know that you can still see me as someone you can be safe with. I need you to know that I would never hurt you. I know that it's a lot to ask, but it kills me to think you may somehow blame me for what happened to you," Devon said, not daring to look at her for fear of what he might see.

"Oh Devon. Even if it turns out to be your father, I could never believe you had anything to do with his actions. I can't explain what I feel about you, but from the moment I woke yesterday knowing that I wouldn't remember you, I still felt safe with you. I know that sounds strange, but I can't help it," Roxie said nervously.

As she said that to him, she knew deep down that it was the truth. She just prayed that she lived long enough to find out about her past.

"Do you think we could start from scratch or would you even want to?" Roxie asked.

Feeling relieved Devon chuckled and said, "Absolutely. I came in here determined to tell you as many stories about our past and anything else you wanted to know to make you feel comfortable around me again."

Smiling at him, Roxie said, "That would be great. I'm getting so bored and I need something to take my mind off everything."

Nodding his head, Devon said, "Okay"

Several hours later and many stories about their childhood pranks, they were laughing when the door opened and Roxie's parents came in. They looked relieved to see their daughter in such high spirits.

"Can we join the party?" Lou asked. He was smiling indulgently as he watched Devon and Roxie together.

Laughing, Devon said to them both, "Of course. I was just telling Roxie about the time that Milly got fed up with your old recliner that you always kept in the living room. Remember the faded blue one? The one that was so worn out it kept the permanent indention of your body?"

Lou laughed fondly at the memory of the chair and then frowned as he also remembered what had happened to it.

Milly was laughing also at the memory until she caught a glimpse of her husband's face.

"Oh Devon," she said. "You would have to be telling that story just as we walked in. You know he still hasn't forgiven me for how I got rid of that chair."

"What did happen to the chair?" Roxie asked.

Trying to keep his laughing to a minimum, Devon continued the story. He tried to avoid eye contact with Lou, although he was sure he could see the shining in Lou's eyes from where he was standing. "Your mom had threatened your dad so many times to get rid of that chair or she was going to do it herself. One day, after one such argument, your dad left to go work out in one of the pastures... building fences or something. Well, Milly got a couple of ranch hands that were working around the barn to come into the house and remove the recliner and she replaced it with a new blue one. Lou had flats on his truck for the next year."

Roxie looked perplexed.

"I don't understand; why would he have flats on his truck from a recliner?" Roxie asked confused.

"I'm sorry, Honey. I forget about your memory sometimes. After the hands hauled it outside, she instructed them to place it in the driveway, which is just dirt and gravel."

"Oh no... she didn't," Roxie said. She understood now, but also wanted to hear the rest of the story, especially looking over at her mother and seeing the blush on her face.

"Yes she did. She set it on fire by pouring a little bit of gas on it and striking a match. The hands realized then that they'd helped her and that Lou probably didn't know what was going on. When the chair was blazing really good, Lou came in from working. He'd forgotten something at the barn. When he finally saw the fire, he ran to the house and was furious that it was his chair was on fire. Well the hands were long gone hiding out and your mother had went back to the house as if nothing had happened."

Pausing for a moment, Devon listened to Roxie's laughter and then finished his story. He wished he could always make her laugh like that.

"Anyway, for the next year or so it seemed he was always getting flats from the nails from that chair."

"Mom, did you ever burn any more of Dad's chairs?" Roxie asked, her eyes shining with amusement.

Sighing, Milly looked at Lou before answering.

"No, but I've wanted to. However, that day I had to promise not to do anything like that again; I mean it's not like I didn't replace the chair with a new one. Your father has always been ungrateful."

"Me? Ungrateful? You burned my chair in the front driveway when I'd left the house. I didn't want a new chair; I wanted that one," Lou said stubbornly. He wouldn't tell her in a million years that he'd dearly loved that new chair. He'd only kept the old one to annoy her, but he'd never admit to it. The old one had been so uncomfortable.

"See Roxie, you'll remember this story for when you get married. Men always sound ungrateful and then they argue like little boys about what they wanted; you'll never win, but you can outmaneuver them, like I did with the chair," Milly said. She was trying not to laugh at the expression that came over Lou's face in that moment.

Looking at Devon, Lou said to him, "Devon, you must always let your wife believe what she wants to believe. It makes for a happier marriage."

Devon and Roxie looked at each other before the laughter got to them and both of them couldn't contain it a second longer.

Laughing so hard that tears came to her eyes, Roxie forced a smile. Roxie wiped them away and said, to no one in particular, "Thank you all for helping me. I feel so much better listening to all the stories Devon's been telling me and the laughter is great."

"That's what we're here for, Honey. Now if you don't mind I'm going to slip out and catch some sleep at home. I'll leave you with your parents. I'll be back this evening," Devon said

"Of course. Go home. I'll be fine, Dev," Roxie said, not realizing that she'd shortened his name like she used to do.

He knew she didn't realize that she'd shortened his name, but it still made him feel good all the same.

"Oh, don't make any plans for this evening," Devon said suspiciously

"Like I'll be going anywhere," she laughed. "What did you have in mind?"

"We have a date," Devon answered. He left before she could ask anything further.

Watching the byplay between their daughter and hopefully their future son-in law, Roxie's parents soon realized that even with her memory loss, Roxie still recognized Devon as her other half, even if she hadn't admitted to it.

Roxie was on cloud nine; Devon was interested in her and they were going to have a date tonight. Thinking about this, she forgot her parents were in the room until she panicked about her clothes. She looked desperately over to her mother.

"You have to help me."

"What's wrong?" Milly asked, anxious all of a sudden. Was there something medically wrong?

"I need clothes for tonight," Roxie said, biting her lip. "Makeup too."

Relieved, Milly smiled.

"Of course. We'll visit for a while and then I'll go shopping while your father stays here with you. You know you still can't leave the hospital, don't you?"

"Yes; that's the reason I need normal clothes. Even if I could leave, I still wouldn't have the strength anyway," Roxie said. She was about to invite them to sit down when the phone rang.

Roxie looked at it nervously, not moving to answer it.

"Do you want me to answer it?" Lou asked. He watched Roxie go from a healthy glow to deathly pale.

Nodding her head, she asked him silently to do just that. She feared it was the man she knew only as "Buddy."

Lou picked up the receiver and asked gruffly, "What?"

Roxie watched as relief washed over her dad and he held the phone out to her with a smile on his face.

"It's Devon."

Taking the phone she said, "Devon, is anything wrong?"

"No," he chuckled. "I'm sorry if I made you think that. I just wanted to tell you something."

Roxie took a breath before asking, "What's that?" She was trying to sound calm.

Devon didn't answer her right away, but then he said quietly, "I love you, Roxie. See you tonight." Without waiting for an answer he hung up. He just hoped he didn't scare her to death with that revelation. I mean it wasn't as if he hadn't told her those words

Eternal Peace

before, but she would remember him now. Oh well, he'd just wait and see. He'd already talked to the doctor and had his date plans okay-ed through him.

Roxie was still reeling from what Devon had just said and was blissfully anticipating her date with him when the phone rang again. This time, not thinking, she picked it up and said teasingly, "Is there anything else you want to tell me?"

"Why yes," said the distorted voice on the phone

Paling for the second time in as many minutes, Roxie choked out, "What do you want?"

"Is Devon Baxter there?" he asked.

Roxie started to say no, but thought better of it.

"He went to the cafeteria," she lied.

Silence met her answer before he said, "You're lying. There's no reason to protect him; it's not like he can protect you."

"What do you mean?" Roxie asked, motioning to her dad. She was hoping he would notify her guard; he took the cue and left.

"Let's just say both your lives are drawing to an end. Now, who to kill first, that's the question." When he got no response he continued, "I think I will kill your boyfriend first and then you; it's not like you're going anywhere anyway."

"You stay away from us," Roxie said, sounding stronger than she really felt.

She heard a distorted laugh over the phone line. It sounded like something out of a horror film and made a shiver race down her spine.

"I know who you are," she spouted in an effort to throw him off.

"Do you now? Interesting, in the end we'll see if you're right," he said mysteriously. He seemed to have lost interest in the conversation.

Roxie looked at her mother who was standing beside her bed. Milly was growing paler by the moment and Roxie imagined she was about the same.

Roxie was getting so tired of his calls because he ended them with her always feeling as if no matter what happened he would always have the upper hand and their was nothing anyone could do about it. She just prayed that the call had been long enough for the FBI to trace, but knew in her heart that it wasn't.

Chapter 20

Roxie was shaking so badly that she barely got the phone back in the cradle. Her mother was resting a hand on her shoulder and asked, "Are you all right, Roxie?"

Trying to stop the trembling in her hands, Roxie looked up and was about to respond when the door flew open and her dad and the two FBI agents came in.

Agents Roberts was the first one to speak.

"Was it him, Roxie?"

Nodding, she let the tears fall freely, managing to say, "Yes; his voice was still distorted, keeping it from being recognized." She went on to tell them the conversation.

"You don't seem surprised that it's John Baxter that has caused all this," she said.

Both agents passed a look between them before answering. Finally, Agent Roberts, the usual spokesman for the pair, said, "No; we've had our suspicions that it is John Baxter."

"Why in the heck haven't you brought him in then?" Lou shouted. His little girl was threatened and there wasn't anything that he could do about it.

"If we could find him we would, but the man is being extremely evasive," Roberts stated.

"Do you at least have any idea on a motive?" Lou asked. He was trying to calm his nerves, but having no success.

"No, we don't know his motive. He may just have snapped after his wife died. With his son being his only relative alive, maybe he wanted to keep Devon cut off from Ms. Lancaster so he sabotaged the Bar B Ranch by stealing the cattle and when people got in the way he killed them. It's all only speculation at this point. All we know is that we need to find him before he kills anybody else," Roberts said.

"Are you sure it's John Baxter?" Milly spoke up. She hated to think that their neighbor and friend of so many years could have anything to do with all the ugliness that had happened.

"All we have is evidence that points in his direction; we need to bring him in for questioning."

"Devon needs to be protected," Roxie said. More and more she was feeling that things were spiraling out of her control.

"We'll go as soon as were done here," Roberts said reassuringly

Roxie knew that it was stupid to bring it up, but she couldn't help it so she said, "We... umm... have a date tonight. Would you please make sure he makes it here, please?"

"Sure, we'll see that he makes it tonight," Agents Roberts assured. He knew that this young woman had been through a lot and just wanted some normalcy in her life; he would do what he could to help.

"Thank you," Roxie said. She was feeling a little stupid that the date was what she was worried about.

The agents left with reassurances that they would do everything in their power to help bring the individual responsible in and to protect both Roxie and Devon.

Hours later, around six in the evening, Devon was whistling as he raced down the stairs. He realized that he'd never told Roxie a time, so he hoped she wouldn't mind him just showing up.

He was about to step out the door for his date when the house phone rang. Devon cursed. He hoped it wasn't Roxie giving him some excuse for calling the date off. Grabbing the phone on the third ring, he shrugged into his jacket to save time and answered, "Hello, Devon Baxter here."

There was a brief moment of silence before the man spoke. Devon was surprised to hear his father's voice.

"Son, how are you?"

"Dad, I've been trying to reach you ever since the night of Wicks' murder. Where are you?" Devon asked desperately. He had temporarily forgot about being in a hurry to meet Roxie for their date.

"I'm around," John said; his voice sounded flat, almost defeated.

"Dad, you have to know the kind of trouble you're in with the law," Devon said. He hated to be the one to tell him.

"I know; there's no help for it," John said

"Dad, you didn't kidnap Roxie did you?" Devon asked, feeling as if he'd ripped out his guts and betrayed his father by asking him.

"Look Devon, I'll explain tonight. I'll be home about ten. Will you be there?" John asked, sounding a bit more stressed as the conversation went on.

"Of course I'll be here. I'm running into town to Peace Co. Hospital to see Roxie for the evening, but I'll make sure I'm here by ten. I need some answers. Your name keeps popping up whenever things happen," Devon said. He didn't want to end the phone call; he was afraid he wouldn't get to ever talk to him again.

"I don't have the time to talk right now. Just make sure you're home at ten tonight," John said and then ended the call.

Devon pulled the phone away from his ear and looked at it like it had grown horns. He then placed it back in the holder mounted on the wall. Not moving for several minutes, he reflected on the strange conversation with his dad.

John Baxter had always been a straightforward man. Evasiveness was out of his character. Devon was very much afraid to think what he was involved in. Glancing at the wall above the back door, he saw the clock and realized that it was now a quarter past six. With the drive into town, he wouldn't have as much time with Roxie as he'd wanted, but he hoped that maybe tonight he'd finally have some answers. He just hoped they were answers that wouldn't wind his dad in jail.

Rushing out the door and to his truck, he stopped just as he was about to step up into the cab. The wind had picked up and it was already dark outside. Maybe he was becoming paranoid, but it almost felt he was being watched. Scanning the immediate area, but not able to see much, Devon brushed it off to being spooked. Nothing was as it should be anymore.

Finally getting in his truck, he turned the ignition. He was feeling suddenly nervous. Instead of just starting up, as it always did, the motor grinded. After a few turns he gave a sigh of relief when the engine turned over. He backed out of his spot beside his house. He needed to get to town before something else happened.

Twenty minutes later he pulled into the parking lot of the hospital. It was now almost seven and he'd only have a little over two hours for their date, but at least it was a start.

Making his way into the hospital, he nodded at the nurses behind their station, but didn't stop to chat with any of them. He had a date to keep in room 110. Seeing the guard posted at the door, Devon saw the man smile as he approached.

"Everything's set up Mr. Baxter; she's waiting for you," the guard said.

Smiling in return, Devon stepped past him to the door.

"Thanks," he said.

Devon didn't bother to knock before he entered. After all, she was expecting him. He was surprised to see her standing by the window. He was even more surprised by her appearance. Roxie hadn't heard him enter so he used the time to look at her. She was in a beautiful light blue dress that clung to her curves, and she had the best curves he'd ever seen on a woman, but maybe he was just partial. Her hair was in a loose braid down her back. He noticed the IV still attached to her hand and smiled. For a minute he forgot that they were in a hospital and that her life was constantly in danger these days. Even with the IV, she looked fabulous.

She was still weak and needed as many fluids in her body that she could get, hence the IV. He didn't know how long he stood there looking at her, but he knew that he'd spend a lifetime doing just that if she'd let him.

He shifted his feet and he saw her turn from the window and look at him. She absolutely took his breath away, especially when a hesitant smile came to her mouth.

"Hi," Roxie said. There was a little catch in her voice as she looked at Devon.

"Hi, yourself," Devon responded.

Roxie was astounded as she looked at him. She thought he was gorgeous before, but she hadn't seen him without that worried, tired look on his face. Tonight he was downright sexy and oozing confidence, and she could tell he must have gotten some sleep while he'd been home. He was wearing a black Cowboy hat, which was tipped back slightly, showing his equally black hair curling over his forehead. She moved her gaze down past his face, which she felt she knew so well from the last few days. She looked his body over.

He had on a heavy leather jacket with a button down shirt that was tucked in a pair of jeans that hugged every part of him. Roxie's mouth felt so dry that she didn't realize that she flicked her tongue out and moistened her lips.

"Roxie," Devon said, almost choking on her name as he saw the assessment in her eyes when she'd looked him over. He'd hoped that the evening wouldn't be too awkward, but she was making it surprisingly easy by showing how attracted she was to him. When she touched her lips with her tongue, he'd almost lost what sanity he had left in him.

Hearing her name, Roxie looked up at Devon's face. She suddenly realized that she'd been ogling him like a treat in a window that she wasn't sure she could have or not.

"Please stop looking at me like that," Devon finally said. He knew that she couldn't remember her past, but it felt like the Roxie he knew that was looking back at him.

Shaking her head, Roxie knew she was acting crazy, but she couldn't help but look at him. She suddenly felt like a different person... or maybe she was just being the way she was normally and simply didn't remember that part of herself. Whatever it was, she didn't want this evening to end. She hoped that by sharing it with him she could recall something of her old self. With that, she turned her sparkling eyes on him with amusement shining in her eyes and asked, "Like what, Cowboy?"

Devon blinked at her calling him 'Cowboy'; Roxie had always used that as a nickname for him for as long as he could remember. Dare he hope that she could remember him and that this was her way of telling him so?

"Do you remember me, Rox?" Devon asked in return. He didn't bother to answer her question.

Roxie looked at Devon and saw the hope shining in his eyes. She knew she was fixing to kill that look.

Sighing before she answered, she said, "No, I'm sorry. What did I say that would make you think that?"

The hope in Devon's eyes dimmed, but didn't go away entirely.

"What you called me. You've always called me that... sort of as a nickname that you used occasionally. You're the only one that's ever called me that, so I thought maybe you were trying to tell me that you remembered me," Devon said.

Roxie saw how disappointed he was that she couldn't remember this one small thing so she tried to give him a little hope by saying to him, "Maybe I do remember you subconsciously and that's why

I said it." She saw by his look and the light that returned to his eyes that she'd said the right thing; she just prayed she wasn't giving him false hope.

He felt foolish that a thing like a nickname could make him feel disappointment, but he also felt better by what she told him about her subconscious probably remembering him, which was most likely just as absurd, but it still made him feel better.

Smiling slightly from her words, he reached up to remove his hat and set it on the small table beside her bed that held the phone. He ran his fingers through his hair.

"I see the food that I ordered was delivered and I wanted to apologize that I was running late for our date," Devon said. He wanted her to know how important tonight was to them both.

She hadn't given much thought as to how this date was going to work until the table, chairs and food arrived. Every little detail made her feel extremely special to this man that she couldn't for the life of her remember.

"It's wonderful that you would do this for me and I didn't mind that you were late," Roxie said, walking to the small table set up in the corner of her room. It truly was a nice setup. There was a little table with a checkered tablecloth set with candles that hadn't yet been lit yet, but soon would be.

Devon came to Roxie and held out his hand so that he could take her to her chair as if they were eating in a five star restaurant and needed to be escorted. He was making her feel terribly romantic and she wondered what their other dates had been like. If any of their past dates had been like this then it was no surprise that she was marrying this incredibly hot man that was also so sweet.

Devon pulled out her chair and helped her get seated, making sure that her IV line didn't snag on anything. He certainly didn't need a nurse rushing in here that would ruin everything; not that this was the perfect date, but it was the only thing he could think of with Roxie not being able to leave the hospital just yet.

Smiling ruefully as he took his own seat he said, "Thanks for understanding." Deep down, Devon knew that she deserved an explanation, but he didn't want to reveal that it was a phone call from his father that had kept him. It wasn't that she wouldn't understand, but he didn't want to upset her either. So he said, "I got held up at my house by a phone call. Unfortunately I'll have to be back home around ten to speak with this person again about some business. I just wanted to apologize ahead of time for leaving earlier than I wanted to."

"It's fine, Devon. That's over two hours for our dinner. I'm sure I will be really tired and not mind when you have to go. Knowing how weak I still am, I'll probably be asleep before you leave. If that happens then I apologize ahead of time," Roxie said laughing.

Uncovering the dishes of food, Devon glanced at her as she spoke.

"Well if you do fall asleep on me then I'll just have to make sure that you're tucked in for the night," he laughed.

Roxie almost dropped her fork when she heard his voice drop to a sexy rumble as he talked about tucking her in. Fumbling to make her fingers work, she scooped a bite of mashed potatoes into her mouth and avoided his gaze, but she heard his deep chuckle as if he knew he was making her uncomfortable.

They settled into their meal and he told her a few more stories about their past. It was such a pleasant meal that she wished it would never end. She was also stuffed. Devon had a heavy meal delivered that had consisted of steaks and potatoes, along with a nice salad and rolls... not to mention the desert that had accompanied the meal.

She was afraid to get up from the table for fear that she would have to waddle back to the bed where she could happily sleep the next eight hours blissfully.

It was past eight and they'd talked most of the time, well he'd talked and she'd listened. She didn't have any stories to contribute, but he didn't seem to mind in the least.

Finishing his latest story, he stood up and walked over to a small radio that was in the extra chair by the door. He turned it on to some soft music that immediately filled the room; it made the atmosphere even more romantic. He turned around and came back to the table with his loose-hipped stride that made her mouth water.

Holding out his hand, he asked, "Dance with me, Roxie?"

She looked from his hand to his face, but didn't take it right away.

"I'm not sure I know how to dance," she said, uncertainty in her voice.

"We're not going to do the jitterbug, Honey. Just sway to the music; I just want to hold you close for a while," Devon said lowering his voice.

Giggling at what he said about the jitterbug, Roxie placed her hand in his and then she remembered her IV and looked questionably at Devon.

"Like I said, nothing adventurous... just a dance. I promise I'll take care of you," Devon assured her. He took her hand and pulled her up against his body.

They didn't do anymore than shuffle back and forth, but it was sheer torture for Devon to hold her this close, breathing in her perfume. He knew that if she'd had her memory he would have already backed her to the bed and slowly lowered her down on it to give her the best pleasure that he could.

Shaking his head to clear his brain, he relished just having her in his arms and simply holding her.

Roxie knew she could get used to this treatment, but couldn't help but wonder about her past with Devon.

Taking a breath and, with her face resting against his chest, she asked, "Devon, what were our past dates like?"

She could feel him tense. She hoped she hadn't said anything out of line, but she was naturally curious about their relationship.

He felt her shift to look up at him, but he pushed her head back to its position resting against him. He took a breath before answering.

"This is our first date, Roxie." He knew the second that he said it she would do a double take.

So if they'd never dated, which was a huge surprise to her, then they must have never had sex. There were so many holes in her mind that needed to be filled. She asked the most embarrassing question. She hated to do it, but she did it anyway.

"Have we ever had um…"She hesitated, not knowing really how to ask that particular question, but Devon luckily took it out of her hands.

He knew where she was going and that she was embarrassed. She smiled at the brief memories and wished she could recall them with him.

"No," he said. "We tried, but something always seemed to happen to prevent it." Amusement rang in his voice and then he felt her shift again. She looked up at him with a puzzled look.

"I can't imagine you having any issues when it comes to me… or any other woman for that matter," she said. She could feel the blush warm her face, so she ducked her head again so Devon wouldn't notice.

Devon felt laughter rumble up from his chest and he couldn't contain it when it came out. He was laughing so hard that he had to stop dancing with her for a second to catch his breath.

"What's so funny?" Roxie asked. She was trying to look hurt that he was laughing at her, but couldn't manage to because she could feel a smile twitching around her own mouth.

"Oh baby, believe me if I got you near a bed when you were healthy enough, I wouldn't have any problems," Devon said. Laughter was still evident in his voice.

Roxie was blushing so badly that she couldn't let him see her face at all. She held it tightly against Devon's chest, but she could feel his body shaking from his laughter and asked, "So what's so funny then? How did we not have sex twice?"

Devon brought his hand up under her chin to make her look at him. He looked into her blushing face and said, "Honey, your parents interrupted us twice or, believe me, you would have already been thoroughly loved by me."

Knowing she would ask, he told her about both incidents and they both were laughing so hard that they'd stopped dancing and were simply standing in one spot holding on to one another.

"Oh you're kidding; that's terrible," Roxie said.

"Both times all I wanted to do was throw your parents out of my house, but they're like my own parents," Devon said.

"Did you mean what you said earlier?" Roxie said, suddenly nervous again around him.

"What?" Devon asked, his mind still on his memories of him and Roxie.

"About loving me?" Roxie said. She didn't bother to look anywhere but at his face. She wanted to see the expression on his face this time.

Devon snapped his attention back to Roxie and realized how much she needed reassurance when she didn't have her memory. All his amusement left as he looked at her.

"Oh Honey; I don't show my emotions very often, but I promised myself after my mother died that if I ever got the chance I would tell you how much I really love you. I wish you could remember the night I proposed to you and told you all that, but if you know nothing else, know that I meant every word to you on the phone earlier. I love you. You're my best friend and my soul mate. With what has happened to you lately, if you feel you can't return the feelings, I'll understand. I'll wait until I earn your love again or until your memory comes back," Devon said finishing on a sigh. He was wondering if he would ever get the chance to have Roxie as his wife.

Roxie could feel tears burning her eyes. She wished with everything in her that she had her memory to remember back so that she could recall their past together. She reached up and circled his neck with her hand. Lightly tugging on his hair, she brought his face close to hers and watched the surprise enter his eyes.

He didn't need much encouragement. He watched her face for any sign that she might pull back at the last second, but she surprised him again by giving another tug and kissing him with such tenderness that he felt it to the end of his toes. He circled her waist with his arms and pulled her closer, but still careful that he didn't hold her too tight.

Roxie was lost in the sensation of Devon kissing her back. She pulled back, slightly nipping on his bottom lip. She didn't want to end the kiss, but she also didn't want to let go of his hand.

Devon opened his eyes and looked down at the slumberous look in Roxie's eyes. He was about to tell her how beautiful she looked, since he hadn't done that yet this evening, but his attention was brought to his phone vibrating in his pocket. Not breaking eye contact with her, he lifted his phone from his back pocket to look at the screen. He suddenly felt all the color leave his face when he saw who was calling. It was almost a quarter to ten; he would be late getting home.

Not bothering to answer his phone, he stuffed it back in his pocket and gently stepped away from Roxie.

"What's wrong, Devon?" Roxie said. She watched the color leave his tanned face and knew that something was suddenly wrong.

"I need to go. Remember earlier I said I needed to leave to be home by ten? Well, that was my appointment calling and it's almost a quarter to ten. I'll be a little late, but he won't mind," Devon said. He hoped she wouldn't ask him any more questions.

"Of course, Devon. I understand. You already explained earlier. Tell whomever you're seeing that it was my fault you were late and that I apologize," Roxie said. She stepped over to her bed and sat down, feeling suddenly weary.

Devon turned to get his jacket off the chair and slip it on, but before he left he looked at Roxie and saw complete weariness on her face.

Stepping over to her, he tipped up her chin to look down into her eyes and said, "I'm sorry, Honey. This evening wore you completely out and now I'm rushing out. I hope you'll forgive me."

"There's nothing to forgive, Devon. I'm tired," Roxie said, not wanting to hold him up much longer.

Devon nodded his head.

"Thank you Honey." Bending down, he lightly kissed her on the mouth and brushed his fingertips down her cheek before turning to leave. At the door, he paused to look back at her and said, "Roxie, I didn't tell you earlier, but you looked absolutely beautiful tonight." With that, he slipped from her room not looking back again. At the time, he didn't realize that if he knew it might be the last time he saw her again, he would've stayed the entire night.

Chapter 21

Devon rushed outside to his truck and pulled his cell phone out again. He dialed the number that had called a minute ago. It was his home phone and could only be his dad trying to reach him. He let the phone ring until the answering machine clicked on and left a message for his dad to pick up, but he never did.

He had a bad feeling about tonight and he had hated leaving Roxie like he did, but he couldn't see any other way. He wanted this whole mess over with and hoped his dad would be the key.

Devon punched down on the gas and his truck lurched forward. He knew he was driving dangerously, but he didn't care. He just felt this overwhelming need to be at his house. Finally, after making the twenty-minute drive in a little over ten, Devon saw the entrance to his ranch and turned the truck up the driveway.

Every light in the house was on, which maybe should have been welcoming, but only made him feel dread in the pit of his stomach. His mouth suddenly became dry. As he approached, he slowed the truck to almost a crawl. He didn't bother parking in his usual spot. He kept the truck closer to the road in case he had to leave in a hurry. *Okay, slow down*, he thought. *Maybe I have watched too many crime shows. I'm becoming paranoid, although four people have already been murdered.*

Devon shook his head and tried to calm himself down. The murders had been gruesome and Devon knew that every time he closed his eyes to sleep he would picture his foreman's face in his mind. He could still see the sightless eyes looking at nothing, but seeing everything all the same. The last thing that Todd Wicks had seen was the person that killed him. Devon couldn't even imagine how terrifying it must have been.

Devon was breathing hard by the time he stopped his truck. He was trying to get the horrible memories out of his mind. He knew that if the killer wasn't stopped, a horrible fate awaited Roxie and he wouldn't allow that. He would lose her again, this time permanently if he didn't do something to stop this madness once and for all.

Devon killed the engine to his truck. He took a minute to look at his childhood home. Taking a deep breath, he stepped around the hood and was about to walk through the front gate of the yard when the most god-awful sound disturbed the unusually quiet night and the ground trembled beneath his feet. He felt a blast of heat so hot that it felt as if he had been thrown in the depths of hell with no chance of escape. His world went black as he was thrown clear over the hood of his pickup to land in a heap on the other side on the ground.

Roxie was exhausted, but couldn't seem to fall asleep so she just laid there in her hospital bed with the TV on, but with the volume turned down low. Her thoughts were still in turmoil and she was getting a headache from it. Although her so-called "date" was wonderful, she was unaccountably depressed all the same. Devon had told her ahead of time that he was leaving, but she still hadn't thought he'd leave as hurriedly as he had.

She knew he would have forgotten about leaving if it hadn't been for that phone call. Maybe he was seeing another woman. She didn't have any memory of him, so how could she really know what kind of man he was? As soon as she had that thought she knew it couldn't be right. For one thing, Devon had lost all the color in his face when he looked at the number calling, which was just as puzzling. Also, he wouldn't have sat with her through the long hours until she'd woken up and taken such good care to make sure tonight was special for her.

But she was worried all the same about him and it all centered on that call that he didn't bother to answer. Maybe he was in some kind of trouble. She knew she would be up all night, not that she could sleep anyway with that man on the loose. Even though there was a guard posted outside, she found she couldn't shut her mind off long enough to sleep.

She glanced at the bedside clock and noticed it was past eleven. Turning back to watch the screen of the TV, she tried to calm her nerves. She almost jumped out of her skin when the phone began to ring. Part of her was terrified that it might be her kidnapper. The other part wanted more than anything to hear Devon's voice on the other end of the line. After a moment of internal struggle, Roxie finally lunged for the phone.

"Hello," she said. There was a shakiness in her voice that she couldn't hide.

Knowing right away that it was going to be an even worse night than she thought, she heard that chilling distorted voice again as he said, "I was just wondering if you wanted to save your fiancé, Roxie?"

Roxie started shaking. She was afraid she was going to drop the phone before she could answer him, but somehow her voice cracked the words out anyway and she asked, "What have you done?"

"The more important question is not what I've done, but what I'm going to do," the voice said, and then he laughed at his own private joke. His laughter sent a chill up Roxie's spine. When she didn't respond, he taunted her by asking, "Come on, Roxie. Don't you want to know what I'm going to do with him?"

Choking on her fear, it took her another few seconds for her to say, "What are you going to do?"

She hated to play his game, but there was no other choice.

"Well why don't you come and find out? Join the party if you will," he said. He was trying to sound persuasive, but only ending up sounding guttural and horrible.

"You don't have Devon. You're just trying to play a mind game with me and I'm through playing your sick game. So why don't you find a cliff, jump off of it and end your misery already?" Roxie said; her voice was rising as anger replaced the fear that was crawling up her stomach. She hoped to God that Devon was at home and not somewhere with this man.

"Well, well. Did you finally find a spine? You just signed his death warrant by not cooperating. His blood will be on your hands and you can live the rest of your life with that guilt on your conscious. Personally, I don't think you're that strong." He paused to let the information sink in before adding, "Now do you want to save him or not?"

Roxie's mind was spinning. How was she going to save him? He needed her; she would do whatever she needed to do to save him. She took a breath and said, "Of course. What do you want from me?"

"Meet me at the Olden place. Don't bring any cops or both of you will die before anyone can say a word. Understand?" he said.

"Yes, but I don't remember anything. How am I supposed to know where this Olden place is?" Roxie said. Her voice was shaking with fear once again.

"Oh yes, the little memory problem. I'll give you directions. I'm sure you're smart enough to get here without arousing any attention." With that, he proceeded to give her the directions she would need. When the line went dead, Roxie just sat there for a few minutes wondering what she was going to do.

First thing she had to do was get the IV out of her hand. She knew that it was going to be painful so, taking a deep breath, she grabbed it and pulled it out. She could feel the tears welling up in her eyes, but she fought them back. With a deep breath, she jumped up and her world began to spin. The next thing she knew she was falling to the floor. She tried to catch her fall, but the side of her face got the bedside table and she almost blacked out from the blow.

She heard the door open and her guard rushed into her room as she was pushing herself back up to stand.

"Ms. Lancaster! Are you all right? Here let me help you," the guard said. He put his hands under her arms and hauled her back to her feet effortlessly. Within seconds she was back sitting her on the edge of the bed.

"Just give me a minute," Roxie said. Her mind was racing with images and memories. Was it possible? Was she getting her memory back? It was almost painful to open her eyes and her brain was overloading all at once with information, plus she was feeling nauseous. She kept her eyes closed until she felt her stomach quit rolling. Somebody was propping her up.

Forgetting about the guard for the moment and why she'd gotten out of bed in the first place, the memory of the call came crashing back. She knew that she needed to find a way to get to Devon. Taking a deep breath again, she opened her eyes and spied the set of keys hooked on the side of the guard's pocket. Putting her hands on his sides, she acted as if she was using him to help her stand, which wasn't far from the truth.

"I'm all right. I was just trying to make it to the restroom when I got up too fast and fell," Roxie said. She was feeling guilty for telling him a lie when he was only trying to help.

"That's okay. Do you want one of the nurses to help you?" he asked, concern in his voice.

"No," she said a little too sharply. He gave her a look and then she said more calmly, "Would it be possible for you to get me some water? I'm so thirsty." Roxie looked at him imploringly. She was hoping that he hadn't noticed the IV that was no longer attached to her hands or the fact that she had slipped his keys off his side.

"I'm not supposed to leave my post ma'am," he said. He really wanted to help her out, but he could get into real trouble if he left.

It cost Roxie to do this, but she took her hand and ran it down the guard's chest. Looking deeply into his eyes and pleading softly, she hoped he would take the bait. She didn't know how long she could keep this up.

"Please," she said.

The guard didn't know what to think. She was definitely a beautiful woman and she didn't seem to mind flirting with him, but she was still extremely weak.

"Okay, I'll go and get you some water. Just promise me you won't try to get up again on your own."

"I promise," Roxie said. She hoped she sounded convincing enough and watched as he turned to leave.

When the door closed, Roxie came off the bed slower this time and let the wave of dizziness disappear before she reached for her sneakers by her chair. Luckily, her mom had brought her some regular pajamas. They were warm flannel ones that would hopefully keep her warm enough. Getting her shoes on, she opened the closet and got her jacket out. She made her way to the door. Before she slipped out she felt for the key ring in her pocket to reassure herself that they were still there.

She opened the door and peered out into the hallway. Luckily it was late and there wasn't anyone around. She knew she needed to get out and past the nurses' station without anybody seeing her, especially that guard. Her head was still pounding after the fall. An onslaught of memories kept going through her mind, but she would deal with that once she got to the guard's car in the parking lot. Hopefully it would be close; she was starting to get really shaky from being up for so long.

Her sneakers were making little squeaky sounds as she hurried down the quiet hallway making her sound extremely conspicuous, but there was nothing she could do about that now. She was starting to sweat from the exertion of not being caught and not being able to sit down. She knew she was racing against the clock.

Finally she came to the corner where the nurse's station was and peeked around the corner only to find it empty. She let out a breath and went past. She was almost to the emergency door when she heard a yell behind her and realized the guard had spotted her down the hall. Taking a breath and breaking into a run (which she barely had enough energy for) she made it outside to the parking lot and ducked behind a car just in time to avoid the guard seeing her.

She watched from around the fender of one of the parked cars as the guard looked around for several minutes calling her name. Eventually he gave an exasperated sigh and went back in talking to someone on the radio attached to his shoulder. Roxie knew she needed to get to his car and out of the hospital parking lot before any cops showed up or the medical staff came outside looking for her.

Raising up and leaning against the car to catch her breath, she scanned all the cars until she located the only car with emergency lights and made her way to it. Taking the ring of keys out of her pocket, she hurriedly looked for the right one. She tried several keys before the fourth one fit the lock on the door. Opening the door, she slid into the seat and rested her head back for a few seconds to help slow her blood from pumping. It felt like she had water rushing in her ears and she was completely out of breath from her escape.

She started the car and tried hard not to touch any of the foreign buttons that probably would turn all the lights on and the siren. She definitely didn't need any more attention focused on her at the moment.

As she made her way out of town, she smiled to herself. She finally remembered that she lived in Peace, Oklahoma, that Devon loved her and that she was ecstatic to marry him.

Eternal Peace

She knew that she would never take her memory for granted again, but she needed to hurry and get to the Olden place. When she was a kid it had been called something different, so somebody must have moved in there for the name to change.

After driving for more than ten minutes and making it out of town without drawing attention to herself, she took a relieved breath and pulled to the side of the dirt road having pulled off the highway a few minutes ago. Her head was pounding badly and the dizziness had come back. She needed to stop driving for a few minutes, catch her bearings and come up with some plan before she made it to the old farm.

Finally with her vision clearing, but still no real plan yet, she pulled back on the road and drove the few miles to the place she was supposed to meet "Buddy". She knew who the man really was, of course, and it made her horrified to think he could lay a hand to hurt her or Devon. It didn't take her long to get to the Olden farm place and she slowly pulled into the yard. It wasn't much to look at, but it was dark and winter. As she began to park the car, she started panicking. She hadn't realized how much the car she was in resembled a police car. *Please don't hurt Devon,* she thought to herself.

Stepping from the car, she looked around the deserted property and remembered the terrible fate that the owners had suffered. The old two-story house was dark and uninviting; the night was very cold with the wind howling through the trees. It was almost saying to anybody listening to leave and not come back. It was an unforgiving place.

Her eyes caught the crime scene tape immediately as she headed towards the front door and it made the evening feel all the more eerie. Spying a faint light coming from within, she placed her hand on the entrance door and slowly pushed inward using what strength she had left. The door was surprisingly heavy. It was made of old timber that was still very solid.

She pushed her way in and lifted her feet over the doorway so as not to trip and bring attention to herself. It was then that she saw him.

It was surreal to her and she dropped to the ground, losing the strength in her body. She was not even able to scream at the sight that awaited her. She started rocking back and forth silently crying for him. She was shaking so badly that she couldn't make it back up from the floor to help Devon down.

Looking up, she heard the swinging of the rope that encircled his feet and prayed he was unconscious and not dead. She still had time to save him somehow. She looked to the floor of the barn and noticed three dark stains that could only be taken for old bloodstains. She forced herself to remain calm. The last thing she needed was to panic. How she was going to help him? She could barely move on her own and felt that she was being watched.

She shifted her body to look behind her and saw only the soulless eyes of her kidnapper.

"Hello John," she said calmly.

"Well, I see someone has her memory back." John Baxter looked down at Roxie taunting her silently with a slight smile on his face.

Chapter 22

Roxie never thought she could feel such absolute hate for another human being, but in that moment all she could feel was anger pulsating through her veins as she looked up into the face of her tormentor.

"Yes I did," Roxie bit out, showing her disgust with him.

"For someone so weak you still have a lot of fire left in you," John said snidely. He put a hand on her upper arm and pulled her to her feet. Shoving her towards Devon he said, "Wake him up. I want him to know what's happening to him when I do it."

"The heck I will. If you're going to kill us then get it over with, you bastard." Roxie's mind was reeling with the fact that the man that had caused so much trouble the last few months was in fact Devon's father, a man that was like a second father to her growing up. Now all she could feel was contempt for him and what he represented.

He advanced on her before she could step out of the way and the slap he delivered to her cheek sent her reeling across the dirt floor. Her body landed in one of the dried bloodstains. Putting her hands under her to lever herself back up, she sat up and felt her lip swelling and the blood that filled her mouth. Spitting out some on the dirt, she looked up at John and spat out acidly, "Who'd you kill here, John? Some more innocent people? Is that is why you brought us here? It's already a crime scene so why waste it, right?"

John Baxter backed up a few steps and an evil little smile shone on his face as he started pacing in front of her; he asked, "The boy that rescued you from the cellar, my cellar, do you remember him?"

Roxie suddenly got a sick feeling in her stomach. "Vaguely. I was almost dead, but yes I do remember a boy helping me. Why?"

He looked at her coldly and said without any emotion, "You're laying in his bloodstain, I believe. Or is that his mother's? Maybe it was his father's? No, it was definitely his. Sometimes it's hard to remember the exact order I put them in."

Feeling her stomach threatening to up heave her dinner from earlier, she crawled away from the blood on the floor and closer to where Devon was hanging several feet off the ground.

"You sadistic bastard!" she screamed. "You deserve to go straight to hell."

"You called me a bastard once before," he said. "Don't make that mistake again or your death will be extremely painful." John stopped his pacing to make his point very clear to her.

Without taking her eyes off of John, she slowly got to her feet and stood beside Devon. Face to face with the love of her life, she was thankful that she could at least tell that he was breathing. She hoped she could find a way to keep him that way.

"Why are you doing this? Why would you hurt your son this way?" Roxie asked.

"He's in my way... just as you are," John said. She was agitating him and he started pacing again, but with more jerky movements. It was if he was thinking too much on how to move his body.

"In your way for what? He's your son for heaven sakes."

"Stop calling him that," John yelled so loud that his voice echoed off the old timbers of the barn scaring a few birds from their nesting places.

"What?" Roxie asked.

"My son," John bit out viciously, turning his back on them both.

"He is your son," Roxie shouted.

"The hell he is!"

"He looks just like you, John. How could you deny the fact that he's your son?"

"Oh he looks just like his father, but I'm not him," John Baxter said. He was speaking in circles.

"So you still despise him after all this time, John?" a voice said from the shadows of the barn.

Roxie whirled around to look at the man stepping out from the darkness. What she saw took her breath away. She looked back at John and saw him staring at the newcomer with such hate in his eyes that it was a wonder the barn didn't collapse around them.

Roxie kept quiet and quickly glanced back at Devon. He was still unconscious.

"You didn't answer my question, brother," the man said. He was keeping his face impassive, but Roxie could tell that there was concern in his eyes whenever he looked in Devon's direction.

"Why should I?" John shouted. "He was never mine." John glanced at Roxie. "I'm sorry for my manners. Meet my brother, my twin brother, James Baxter," John said, his voice dripping with sarcasm.

Roxie was stunned. The resemblance was so uncanny that she was speechless. She felt the hot breath of Devon on her neck and turned slightly towards him, keeping her eyes locked on the two opposing men.

Lifting her hand up to Devon's face, she gently stroked his cheekbone and said to the Baxter twins, "He needs to be cut down and helped." Rationally Roxie knew they wouldn't help her, but she was frantic to get Devon down, especially since the only thing in the barn was old hay and bloodstains. There was nothing sharp or even metal lying around that she could use and she was afraid to leave Devon unprotected so Roxie waited, praying John would forget this madness or that James Baxter would help them. John snorted and said, "Not likely; he stays where I put him. Besides, now that I've got the three people here that I want rid of the most we can complete my plan. No one is going anywhere."

"Son or not, you wouldn't actually hurt Devon, would you?" Roxie asked, her voice quivering. He didn't let her finish her thought before cutting her off.

"He's not my son and I don't give a damn if he lives or dies," John said, his face turning an ugly red. He pulled a large knife from a scabbard hidden underneath his jacket and lightly slapped the flat side of the blade against his side.

Roxie was stunned that this man could be so callous and unfeeling. Her mind filled with a million memories of her past... of her and Devon growing up. John had never been cruel to either of them, but definitely hard. What had happened to make him snap like this? She wished Devon would wake up. More than anything she hoped he wasn't seriously injured. He didn't seem to have any visible wounds, but his clothes were filthy. She smelled the faint odor of smoke.

Roxie's eyes were focused on the knife that John was clutching in his hand, but she could see James moving out of the corner of her eye. He slipped something from the inside of his jacket and caught her eye. Hoping she had some help in this stranger, she started trying to wake Devon up.

She hated the fact that he would find out about his father, or rather who his real father was, this way; either way it was going to be devastating to him.

"Devon," Roxie said, still lightly stroking his cheek. She kept saying his name over and over again, willing him to wake up. She kept staring back and forth between Devon and the two brothers who were still in a heated conversation.

"Then why did you raise him all this time if you didn't so much as give a damn if he lived or died? Why do all this now?" James demanded.

John looked at his twin for several minutes before he answered, "Because the only person I ever cared about is gone; Lilly was the only reason I kept up the charade that Devon was my son."

Devon could hear voices, angry voices, talking over the ringing in his head, but couldn't quite make out the words. He felt like all the blood had settled in head, making it feel like it was literally going to explode, then he felt the light caress on his cheek and what he thought was his name being said over and over as if trying to get him to open his eyes.

His eyelids felt like they were glued together and he wondered what in the hell had happened to him to give him such a headache. Maybe he'd finally gone over the edge this time and drank himself into oblivion, but if he was this drunk then why did everything feel horrible? He should be feeling no pain.

Then it all came crashing back to him, as if his life was flashing by. Everything that had happened in the last few months rocked through his brain, stopping with him pulling up in front of his house and being launched through the air, then nothing but blackness until now. Oh god, his father was supposed to have met him at home. He must have been in the house when it exploded.

Devon tried again to open his eyes, then realized he was completely immobile. He couldn't move his legs or arms. Feeling trapped, his eyes shot open as he began to struggle. His vision was blurry and his head still felt as if a buzz saw was cutting through it.

Roxie was so relieved to see Devon starting to struggle that she almost forgot to calm him down so he wouldn't hurt himself further. His eyes fluttered open.

"Devon can you hear me?" Roxie asked.

Devon finally could focus enough to see Roxie standing a matter of inches from his face, but he didn't understand what was going on. She was upside down. No wait, he was the one upside down. He was so confused and he could hear her say something, but then he looked past her to the man standing slightly behind her and realized it was his dad. All he could feel was relief that he was alive.

He looked back at Roxie. He couldn't understand what she was doing outside of the hospital.

"Are you all right, Rox?" he asked.

Roxie felt tears sting her eyes. After all Devon had been through, he was still concerned about her first. She nodded her head; there was no way she could trust her voice.

Devon knew he was in big trouble when he realized that his body was swinging upside down from the rafter of an old barn. He noticed the other man and was stunned to see a double of his father.

"My vision is a little off," he said uncertainly. "I'm seeing double, but then why wouldn't I see two of you also? My head hurts so bad and why am I tied up?"

"Look who finally decided to wake up," John said.

Focusing on his dad, Devon said thickly, "Dad, what's going on? I thought you were in the house when it exploded."

Laughing cruelly, John looked at the man that he'd raised and said, "I'm not your father; he is." John pointed at James and Devon fought the overwhelming sense of confusion that he was feeling.

"What are you talking about? I look just like you. Of course you're my father," Devon said. He was becoming extremely uncomfortable being upside down. He could feel the circulation in his legs being cut off and knew he needed to get down quick.

"Well I never thought you for an idiot, so I assume you've seen the man that looks exactly like me. Meet my twin brother, James. He's your father." Before Devon could dispute anything, James spoke up.

"I can't believe you are so stupid that you don't think he's your son," he said in complete exasperation.

"Enough of this. I'm tired of all this reminiscing," John said. To everyone's astonishment, he threw the knife straight at Devon.

Devon felt the white-hot pain of the blade pierce his chest. Blood gushed out the wound and flowed down to his shoulder. He could vaguely hear Roxie scream as blood spattered her face. She was pressing her hand around the sides of the blade trying to stem the flow of blood.

"Oh god Devon, don't you die on me! I'll get you out of this, I promise," Roxie screamed. She was starting to panic at the amount of blood pumping out of him and between her fingers. Suddenly she jumped. There was a gunshot followed closely by two more before she dared look behind her. There was John Baxter lying in the dirt. He was looking up at his brother with a mixture of shock on his face.

"You idiot! You probably just killed your son!" James was shaking violently. He had placed his shots well enough to keep his brother alive. He desperately needed answers. Holding a hand to his shoulder wound, John tried to get up, but couldn't. He'd been shot in both legs, causing him to crumple to the dirt and have to look up at his brother. He didn't think James had it in him to shoot his own blood. Then he saw the cell phone that James pulled from his pocket. James was calling for an ambulance.

So his darned brother was a stupid cop; wasn't that just everything he needed at the moment?

"I told you he's not my son," John said repeating himself.

"Why do you think that?" James demanded. He was still clearly puzzled and, knowing they didn't have much time before Devon bled out from his wound, he continued to question. He wasn't going to leave until he finally understood what was going on.

"Because I saw you all those years ago. I saw you coming out of Lilly's bedroom at her parents' house before we were married. I saw how close the two of you were and that you wanted nothing more than to sleep with her... and you did," John spat out.

"You fool!" James exclaimed. "I never slept with Lilly." Shock was written all over James' face. He couldn't believe that his brother had felt this way for so many years and had never confronted him about it.

"The hell you didn't."

"Did you ever ask Lilly?" James asked quietly. It was true. He had been in love with Lilly for years, but he had never made a move. He didn't realize that he would lose his brother either way.

"No. She would've just lied to me so I pretended that nothing happened between the two of you, but when the boy was born I knew he wasn't mine. I could never get close to him. I resented him, but I hid it well from Lilly. I think she always suspected something, but we never talked about it," John said. He could feel all of his strength leaving his body along with all of his blood that was pooling around his wounds.

James shook his head.

"I never knew you thought this," he said. "Lilly and I would have straightened you out years ago because the simple fact is that Devon is your son, not mine. Believe me, if I'd thought he was mine and I'd known what you were truly like you would never been allowed to be around him."

Roxie and Devon had listened to every word of their conversation. It was the only thing keeping Devon conscious at the moment. He still couldn't believe what he was hearing. Who was his real father?

Then Devon felt his body start to shake and the blackness began to invade his vision. The last thing he saw was Roxie's face before he succumbed to the loss of blood and passed out.

"Help me!" Roxie screamed. "He's going to die!"

"I'll cut him down," James said, hurrying to her side, "but you're going to have to help lower him to ground. Get him as comfortable as possible until the ambulance gets here." After Devon was lowered to the ground and the ropes were removed from his ankles and wrists, they could hear the sirens in the distance and Roxie looked at James across Devon's body and asked hopefully, "Will he make it?"

"I don't know, Honey," James said looking down at his nephew with affection and concern.

"Are you a cop?" Roxie asked. She was trying to keep her mind off the situation, but she didn't move her hands from their firm place on Devon's chest.

Devon's uncle chuckled. He sounded so much like Devon that Roxie couldn't; help but feel a bit better. His response made her feel even better. "I'm with the FBI actually. I think you met a couple of my agents, Roberts and Hillman."

As she looked at him, she remembered her impression of the resemblance between the brothers. Even though they were identical, they definitely weren't the same and she was so relieved to have all this behind her. She still didn't really understand John's motive in killing innocent people. What was the purpose?

"This still doesn't make any sense to me," Roxie said to James as they heard the emergency vehicles come to a stop outside the barn. "Why would he do all this?"

"I don't know. He'll live; on the way to the hospital I'll get the reasons out of him. It still doesn't make sense to me either. In fact, he was the contact for my agents when you went missing because I needed someone I trusted in the area. I never dreamed he was the one that kidnapped you and killed these people or would try to kill Devon," James said, standing up as the paramedics rushed in. He left Roxie standing alone as he hurried over to speak with the police.

Roxie could tell they needed to get Devon to the hospital; his skin was already losing what color it had and he looked close to death, especially when his breathing became so shallow it was hard to hear him. As they loaded him in the ambulance, Roxie reached out and took his hand. She kept talking to him hoping he would hang on for her.

As they arrived at the hospital everything passed in a blur. There seemed to be people everywhere and someone was always trying to take her away from Devon, but she screamed at them saying she wasn't leaving his side; he would die without her. Then she saw the guard that was assigned to watch her room come into the emergency room and spot her. Walking towards her, he threw her over his shoulder and took her back out in the hallway, not bothering with her protests.

"Stop, you're just getting in the way," the guard said. He was trying to be soothing. "Come on, I can tell you're not going back to your room. At least let a nurse look you over and then I'll wait in the waiting room with you until you hear something, okay?"

Roxie was stressed out, but she looked at him and knew he was right. Without saying another word, she nodded and let him lead her to a curtained area where a nurse was waiting to look her over.

James told her later that Devon and John had been taken to surgery. James had finally gotten the entire story out of his brother and was even more shocked by his cruelty. He couldn't believe they were related to each other. He hadn't said anymore about it, knowing that they both wanted to forget about the tragic incidents that had happened lately and focus on waiting for Devon to get out of surgery. They both knew they would have to face it later. Roxie wasn't even sure she wanted to know why John Baxter had gone crazy. All she wanted was this awful mess to be behind her.

After what seemed to be hours, the door opened and one of the doctors came in, his scrubs covered in blood and a look of dejected weariness on his face.

Instantly, Roxie started shaking. She knew that whatever the doctor had to say it wouldn't be good. She could feel the tears start to fall down her face as he started to speak.

"I'm sorry we did everything we could, but Mr. Baxter didn't make it."

Chapter 23

Seeing Roxie starting to get hysterical, James asked, "Devon Baxter or John Baxter?"

The doctor, realizing his mistake, said hastily, "John Baxter."

Roxie realized that she'd immediately thought it was Devon because she'd honestly blocked out John Baxter, only wanting to concentrate on Devon and his injury. Feeling relieved, she looked up suddenly angry.

"Good. He needs to rot in hell for what he's done!" As soon as she said it, Roxie covered her mouth with her hand and saw the shocked expression on the doctor's face. She slowly looked to her side at James Baxter to see the hurt look on his face.

Removing her hand, she immediately apologized, but James waved her away.

"It's okay. He was my brother, but he'd turned into something I didn't recognize over the years. I'll grieve, but it'll be for the man he was... not what he became."

"I'm still so sorry," Roxie said hating that her anger got the better of her.

The doctor cleared his throat to get their attention.

"John Baxter died on the table from a heart attack and we were unable to revive him. Devon Baxter, however, is going to be fine. His wound was very deep, but somehow missed anything vital. He did lose a large amount of blood though and he'll be here at least a week."

"Can we see him?" Roxie asked. She was feeling more relieved now than she had for the last few hours or, for that matter, the last few days.

"Yes, but only for a few minutes. Follow me," he said. Before checking to see if they were following, he left. As they entered Devon's room, Roxie walked up to his bed and laid her hand on his arm stroking it to see if he was awake.

"Devon, can you hear me?"

Moaning, Devon shifted and then winced, but he opened his eyes to see Roxie bending over him.

"Roxie," he mumbled.

"I'm here Dev," Roxie said. She squeezed his hand to reassure him.

"What's going on?" Devon asked. He needed to know if his father had really been the one to cause so much destruction.

"Devon, we only have a few minutes and you need to rest so we'll explain everything when you're more alert," Roxie said hoping he wouldn't push the issue. She looked behind her, but James had opted to stay by the door. He just wanted to make sure that Devon was truly all right. He didn't say a word. There would be plenty of time for talking and he didn't relish that conversation.

Roxie looked back at Devon and saw that he'd already slipped back into to sleep.

A week later Devon had been released from the hospital and Roxie had brought him to her parents' house to recover. The Baxter house had been blown up. James was meeting them at Roxie's parents' place to finally explain to everyone what had caused John Baxter to do what he did. It was the first time Devon would officially get to meet his uncle.

Roxie helped Devon to the loveseat in the living room and laughed at her mother who was flitting around trying to make sure

Devon had everything he needed. She was making him feel like an invalid. Devon just wanted to get this over with and never think of his father again.

Watching the expressions on Devon's face as she settled down next to him, Roxie asked, "Are you all right, Dev?"

"I'm fine," Devon said. He was thinking back to when he'd woken in the hospital. He had thought it was a dream when she'd been there waiting by his bed. When he finally found out what had happened from her, he sat in shock for hours and after the shock had worn off she'd gently told him about his father and that she had her memory back.

Devon was thankful for Roxie's parents. They'd been great ever since he was kid, but had especially helped him from the time of his mother's funeral until now, letting him stay until he could rebuild his house. Lou and Milly Lancaster would always be considered two of his favorite people, besides Roxie that is.

Roxie felt Devon tense when they all heard the knock on the front door. As James Baxter entered, Roxie heard Devon suck in a painful breath as he watched a duplicate to his father walk in the room. His father had been buried a few days earlier and Devon hadn't been able to go to the service. Roxie doubted that he would have gone if he'd been able to. He had simply asked Roxie to take care of all the preparations.

James Baxter came into the room and immediately saw the tension on his nephew's face. He wished that Devon were his son. He gave a nod at Lou Lancaster and his wife, having met them earlier in the week. He took a seat across from Devon and Roxie and prepared for their questions, but hoped they would just let him tell them what he knew and let that be the end of it.

James could tell that it was extremely painful for Devon to look at him.

He started his story the only way he knew how... he just jumped right in. "Roxie, it was a fluke. You weren't involved at all; you just came home at the wrong time. John's mental state was unstable for years, but he didn't fully snap until Lilly died. This next part will be hard. Whatever his reasons were, I can honestly tell you they were unfounded," James said sincerely. Devon was holding back tears, but he clearly looked upset.

Seeing Devon get under control without anyone else noticing the slight pause, James went on to say, "Your father believed that Lilly and I had an affair at the same time that he was dating her; we weren't, but he was convinced. She got pregnant, but I swear I had nothing to do with it. Even though I loved Lilly I never slept with her. John was your father, but he truly believed that he wasn't. He didn't want to lose her by throwing around accusations, so he kept quiet. I can only guess that the relationship between the two of you was always very strained. Am I right, Devon?"

Nodding his head, but not answering with words, Devon looked down at his hands and then concentrated on Roxie's fingers entangled with his. He knew that if he had nothing else, at least he still had Roxie. He'd hold on to that. Looking back up for his uncle to keep going, he listened in silence.

"Thought so," James said. "He said as much. John said he resented you because he thought that you were really my son. I want to apologize now, Devon. If I'd known what was going on I would have confronted him, but after John and Lilly got married I just couldn't be around, so I left. After Lilly died, John left to make plans to get you out of his life forever. He wanted to live on the ranch as if you'd never existed. He told me about paying the foreman Todd Wicks extra cash to try and kill you, but to make it look like an accident. "Your cattle are on the place that your father had rented in his absence from the ranch; they've already been returned to your pasture," James said.

James looked from one person to another. He knew that he was looking at two people that loved each other very deeply.

Devon was having a hard time taking all of this in, but he finally worked around the lump in his throat to ask, "The explosion at my house? He was hoping I'd be there. I was supposed to be home by ten to meet him and we were going to talk, but I didn't know what about. I thought he would help me find out who was doing this. I was hoping he would tell me he had some evil twin or something." The second the words left his lips he realized how ironic the statement was. His father, not James, was the evil twin in this story.

"So how was it you knew where we were?" Roxie asked. "Were you already in the barn?"

"Well my agents were starting to have suspicions about John and after a lot of deliberation they finally called me for advice. I'd given them John's name as a contact on Roxie's kidnapping case because he was familiar with the area, but they also knew he was my brother. Knowing that they didn't want to implicate him without proof, the investigation went on. They decided it was best if they told me everything. I came down personally to handle the rest of the case. I was hoping that somehow something got screwed up somewhere, but soon came to realize that when I couldn't reach him myself or find him, that things had gone wrong. I had Roxie's phone in the hospital bugged when he called you and gave you directions to the Olden place.

"Fortunately for all us he hadn't arrived by the time I got there. He must have called you as he was leaving Devon's place. So I got there ahead of everybody, but waited until Roxie arrived so that hopefully I'd have a conscious witness," John finished. "The rest you know." Everybody was silent for several minutes before Devon finally spoke.

"Will you take me to his graveside?" he asked his uncle, not looking at anyone else in the room. Devon knew that James would understand without him having to say anything more.

Looking back into his nephew's green eyes that were so much like his own, James slowly nodded. He realized that Devon needed to release his grief without anybody around. Roxie didn't let go of Devon's hand, but asked, "Are you sure, Dev?"

"I need to do this," Devon said looking down at her. He hoped that she would understand and not be hurt that he hadn't asked her to go.

"Okay, Cowboy. Do what you need to do. I'll be here waiting for you," Roxie said. She released his hand and let it slip away.

Arriving at Peace Cemetery on the outskirts of the town, Devon slowly got out of his uncle's car and followed him to the graveside.

After walking for a few minutes, James stopped at the newly turned earth that marked the grave. Stepping to the side to give Devon more space, James said, "I'll give you a few minutes alone."

"No, stay," Devon said. He didn't really want to be completely alone as he said goodbye to his father.

"Okay," James replied. He didn't say anything else.

Devon took a breath and was about to say something meaningful, or at least thought he was, but all that came out was, "Goodbye, Dad." Then Devon noticed what was written on the headstone and read it aloud.

"May you find eternal peace in your final resting place."

Looking over at his uncle James with tears silently coursing down his face he said, "Thank you for putting that on his headstone; it fits. I hope he does find peace. It's ironic that he lived in a town named for it, but he never found it here. I don't know if I can ever forgive him, but he was a part of my life for so long that I needed some sort of closure." Wiping his face before turning from the grave and going back to the car, Devon turned and walked away. He never came back to the cemetery even though his father was buried next to his mother.

Epilogue
One Year Later

Devon hadn't thought this day would ever get here. Roxie had gone into labor two hours ago and since she was having a C-section (because the doctor had worried about some complications) he was stuck in the waiting room with his in-laws and his uncle, James.

He smiled at the memory of the last twelve months. Soon after the misery of last year it hadn't taken long for Devon to remove all the debris from his old house and set into motion the new home that he had built; it was a two-story ranch house that he let Roxie decorate. He'd also loaded Roxie on a plane and married her in Vegas. Then he took her to New York to quit her job and move all her things back home with him, making sure this time that she did in fact come back. He was a man that took no more chances in life. Life was way too short.

He'd also developed a close relationship with his Uncle James, who felt more like a father to him with each passing day. Devon had even asked him shortly after he'd gotten married if he had any life advice to give because he'd felt that was what a son was supposed to ask a father. He'd laughed at the time about the advice, but now didn't think it was so funny.

Eternal Peace

That day after Devon had asked, James had looked him dead in the eye very seriously and said, "Pray that when you and Roxie have kids, that you don't have twins."

Now almost nine months later, they were having twins and Devon wasn't smiling anymore.

THE END

Acknowledgments

To my husband, Cliffton for putting up with me while I was writing, thank you honey. To my sister-in-law Margie and my sister Sandy for reading my first rough draft and believing it could get published. To my parents Don and Vicky for knowing and believing I could do anything. With all my love to my family for supporting me in my dreams, bless you all.

Also thanks to my very wonderful editor Katie Fawkes for helping me through the editing process and being a huge support to me when it all seemed overwhelming. Of course special thanks to the wonderful staff of American Book Publishing for helping a dream come true.

About the Author

Stephanie Owens was born and raised in Southeastern Oklahoma earning her degree at Southeastern Oklahoma State University in Business Administration. Having worked in the banking industry for four years and earning her certification in Internal Auditing, she is now writing and enjoying herself immensely.

Besides her love of writing she lives on a ranch with her husband Cliffton and together raises longhorn cattle. When she's not writing she can be found enjoying a good book, riding horses, team roping, or working on her many projects around the house.